I'd like to thank my wife, Julie, and my son, David

I0548435

Books by Tony Marvin

The Templar Chronicles Series
Betrayal – Darkness Engulfs the Knight
Fugitives – Stripped of the Cross
Dispersion – Dawn of a New Knight

Science Fiction
The House on Crescent Street

Action-Adventure
The Making of a MERCYnary

Cover Art and Website development by
LDerrickson Digital
www.Derricksondesign.com

Published by
Pen and Steel

1

Book 2 of the Templar Chronicles
Fugitives
Stripped of the Cross

Introduction

Letter sent to the baillis and seneschals on September 14, 1307,
ordering the arrest of the members of the Order of the Temple.

*"A bitter thing, a lamentable thing, a thing which is horrible
to contemplate, terrible to hear of, a detestable crime, an execrable
evil, an abominable work, a detestable disgrace, a thing almost
inhuman, indeed set apart from all humanity."*
This is the opening of the letter that called for the arrest of
the Templars in France to be carried out on Friday, October 13,
1307. Against all the odds, the raid went off almost perfectly.
Historical records indicate that in France, a few notable Templars
escaped the initial round-up, but most were later captured. At least
that is how the story is usually told. No one truly knows the exact
number of Templars in France or in any other European locations at
the time of their arrest. There were plenty of forewarnings that King
Philip of France, along with Guillaume de Nogaret, the king's
advisor, was planning something of this nature. If there were
Templars left free, what happened to them? We know that after their
arrest and "confession," a few were allowed to join other monastic
Orders, such as the Hospitallers. In some countries, the Templars
were left largely unharmed until the Pope suppressed the Order in
1312. In Portugal, the Templar knights based there were entirely
reorganized as the Order of Christ in 1319. Many have asked what
became of their wealth, their fleet of ships, and whether there were
more of the warrior monks who were never captured? History has
provided no clear answer, and therefore, we assume that the few who

remained free merely crept into obscurity. I do not think men of the caliber of what we know of the Templars would do well simply letting life pass them by. These were not men who rode the current of the river of life. These were men who fought against it and then built structures to direct and harness the river's flow.

Chapter 1

They had laid the boards on sawhorses to make a large table. Father Lull and Commander of the Vault of Acre, Admiral Gregory, began to lay out the twelve sheets in their proper order. They carefully placed stones at the corners to hold them in place. When they had it completed, the Admiral of the Templar fleet stood below where the westernmost part of the World was; this placed China at the top of the map.

"This is the way most maps are positioned with China at the top," Gregory said almost to himself as he studied the huge image of the world before him. Sir William Knight of the Temple and his squire Louis stared uncomprehendingly at the images drawn out on the paper. A few of the Latin words written on the map were familiar to them, but they could not orient themselves well enough to make heads or tails of the locations depicted. Father Lull seemed to be lost in thought as he also studied the map, slowly walking around the table.

Admiral Gregory said, "It says down here in the corner that the map was copied from one of the Chinese leaders, The Great Kublai Khan. The map was copied from one that hung in one of the Khan's many palaces. It appears the trader who copied it translated the Chinese writing into Latin, which is quite helpful to us." The Admiral was then quiet again as he studied the map.

Finally, Father Lull said to Gregory, "Can this be accurate? It clearly is unlike most European maps, which are more works of art rather than something meant to truly portray the World, but if this is supposed to be accurate like the charts you sailors use, and it is to be believed, then..." Father Lull trailed off, lost in thought and study.

After a moment, Admiral Gregory replied, "I think we are to take this as a true representation of the World. At least, how the Chinese believe the world to be. I think it is a much more detailed portrayal of the World than what we have previously seen. Look here at the top, we have China, and over here is India."

Father Lull interrupted and excitedly said, "Do you see what it says there near India? It shows the 'Kingdom of Prester John.' Do you think this is where we could find the great Christian leader and his army that would help us retake the Holy Lands?"

Gregory, continuing as if he had not heard the father, "Here is Europe, which would be at the bottom on our maps, but this map shows more below. There appear to be several large islands to the West of Europe and Africa. It would be a long way to sail over the open ocean, but this map does not include the lands to the North. Germany is hardly illustrated, and Norway is not included, nor is Greenland. Iceland, sometimes referred to as Thule, is also missing. I think it might be possible to sail to Norway, then onto Iceland and Greenland, and continue Southwest to this large island."

Father Lull said, "Are you sure we have assembled the pages correctly? I wonder if these bottom pages are supposed to go at the top."

Gregory said, "It is laid out correctly, and you are right, they could be placed at the top. There are markings in all the corners that we sailors use on our charts to indicate their location relative to other charts in our collection. See here." Gregory lifted a stone to show the markings in the corners. "The marks on this bottom row of sheets indicate they can be connected to the bottom of this side or the top of the other. That way, we can get a flat view of the spherical World."

"Spherical World? What are you talking about?" Sir William asked.

Father Lull looked at him and said, "Yes, William. You must know the World is a ball. You are not one of those idiots who believe the Earth is flat, are you?"

William, noticing everyone was staring at him, including Louis, replied rather hesitantly, "Well...I guess I never really thought about it."

Father Lull, noticing William's embarrassment, said, "I'm sorry, I didn't mean to imply that you are an idiot. Not being a sailor like Admiral Gregory here or someone who has spent a great deal of time studying maps and charts like me, of course, you may have never thought about the shape of the Earth, but trust me, the Earth is a sphere. The Ancient Greeks proved it and even developed a few calculations to determine its circumference. If we use Eratosthenes' calculation, which I find incredibly elegant and sound in its design, then the Earth is much larger than many people today believe. Thus, making it very likely that there are large land masses we have yet to discover. Perhaps the very land masses this map indicates"

Master Gregory interrupted and said, "The lad's likely to find himself at sea with me soon enough, then he can see for himself how other ships and land rise as you approach them over a flat, calm sea. Or I'll send him up the mast and give him a clear, unobstructed view where he'll see for himself how the horizon curves away to both sides."

William, wishing to change the subject, said, "That would be quite interesting to see. You had mentioned earlier that maps in Europe are often not intended to be accurate. What are they for if they are not accurate? I thought maps showed where distant places were, so you could travel to them."

Gregory said, "No, most maps contain only the vaguest resemblance to what the true world looks like. If we used them to guide us, there's no telling where we might end up. Sailors use charts to help navigate. Most of our charts are drawn by us, and we guard them very closely. Occasionally, some old salt may retire from years at sea and hand over his charts to a son or close friend, but mostly we trust only our own drawings and notes."

Louis asked, "If the maps are not to show where places really are, what are they for?"

Father Lull said, "They serve other purposes, sometimes they are just decorations that a Monarch pays some artist to create to show all that he rules over." With a smile on his face, he added, "Amazingly, the kingdom of the Monarch who pays for the map is always much larger than any other province on the Monarch's map.

"Some maps are to help people understand that the world is bigger and more amazing than the little piece of it they see, since few common people travel very far from their homes. Of course, the Church uses maps to help teach truths about the Faith. Most maps in

Europe show China at the top and the western coast of Europe at the bottom. In these maps, although it is not entirely accurate, Jerusalem is placed in the center. This is done to teach Spiritual ideas. For instance, we believe that Eden was located in the far East, where wisdom originated. Wisdom then started to move West in the same direction that the Sun travels.

"Some theologians believe that once wisdom has fully arrived in the West, then Gog and Magog will rise, and the world will end. Some people in the Church already believe that wisdom has reached its ultimate level and there is nothing new to learn. They believe knowledge is now dominated by us in the West. Therefore, they presume that the end is upon us. Many believed Gog and Magog would attack in 1250, and they were honestly disappointed when it didn't happen. Every few years, someone comes up with a prophecy or calculation they have made that predicts the end of the World. They're all very lucky the Church doesn't follow Old Testament laws about false prophets any longer, or these men would be stoned to death. I'm sorry, I have gotten off-topic. I tend to drift occasionally when I get in a teaching mode."

Gregory snorted and said, "Ha, 'occasionally'? That's a good one. What the good Father is trying to say is that most maps aren't worth a shit if you want them to find some real location. This one, on the other hand, has the look of a true chart. If I were to compare this map to the same locations depicted in my charts, I can tell you right now they would be amazingly similar. This map shows a great deal more of the world and has much more detail than all my charts combined. My charts focus on coastlines, but this shows detailed features hundreds of miles inland. For the portions I know, this appears to be to scale. Truly amazing. The Chinese must be great world travelers and explorers."

Louis chimed in, "I appreciate that this map must be something special, but was it so important that Sergeant Bertrand should have lost his life protecting it? It's interesting, I guess, but what good is it really?"

Gregory looked at the squire and was about to say something, changed his mind, then turned to Father Lull and said, "I've no patience for this, you talk some sense into them. I'm going to get my chartbook and start copying this. I've got the feeling you're going to want to put these back in their tubes, reseal them, and secret them away soon. And before they disappear again, I want to get a copy I can use."

Father Lull turned back to William and Louis and said, "I understand this cannot seem as valuable as a man's life, but this map may save many men's lives. All the Templars in France are fugitives of the Crown of France. The way things are progressing, I am reasonably certain that soon the Pope Himself will force the other Monarchs to follow suit, and there will be no safe location in all of Christendom for any Templar. This map may provide a haven where the Order can consolidate its strength and reestablish its innocence of all these charges."

William asked, "Where would that be, Father? Are you suggesting we go off searching for Prester John? Or sail into unknown parts of the World looking for a new home? Won't we look even more guilty if we run away? We should approach the Pope and make our stand directly with the Holy See. Then the Pope can talk some sense into King Philip."

Father Lull thought for a moment, "I do not know what direction the Templar Order should take, but I would not rule out either option of seeking out Prester John or lands unknown to us. Other men will make that decision. Going to the Holy Father is no longer an option. Although I have not heard of an official ruling, King Philip and Guillaume de Nogaret, his advisor, have made a compelling case in the public eye, which would likely deter the Pope from forcing them to release the Templars at this time. We need to seek a long-term solution. We will have to prove the Templars' innocence. Which will be difficult with the confessions King Philip's tortures have already extracted. We will need to demonstrate that the King and Guillaume de Nogaret carried out these arrests to seize the Templars' money and lands, and to avoid repaying the money the Crown of France had borrowed from the Templars.

"In the short term, you two are going to head to Scotland. In the letter Grand Master Jacques de Molay sent with you, he included the instructions to send your party on to whatever safe location outside of France that Jon, Seneschal of the Templars, has sent other Templars to."

William said, "Scotland? What can we do there? Isn't that all just a bunch of hills with sheep farmers living there?"

Father Lull smiled and said in a humorous tone, "Yes, just a bunch of mild sheep farmers…you will soon be their guest along with several hundred other knights, sergeants, and squires of the Temple who are already there."

Chapter 2

Mary and Derrick had walked along the road leading south for several days. They kept to themselves, and since, at a glance, anyone who met them assumed they were a couple of men of no consequence, no one bothered them. By the third day, Mary began to grow uncomfortable with the added bulk she had on under her clothing to hide her woman's figure. She repeatedly had to stop, step into the woods, and readjust something that had come untucked, or loose, or had started to sag.

Even with the occasional stops, they kept a good, steady pace. At first, Mary had trouble keeping up with Derrick, who always seemed to walk with a purpose. Soon, Mary grew used to the daily routine of rising before the sun, eating a quick cold breakfast, and walking all morning until the sun rose high overhead. Then they would eat lunch while walking through the afternoon. About an hour before dark, they would walk far enough into the woods so that no one would bother them. Derrick would start a small, cheerless, and mostly smokeless fire, and they would eat and chat a little before going to sleep.

They didn't talk much while they were on the road, fearing that someone might hear Mary and realize she was a woman, not the man she appeared to be. However, when they were off in the woods, they would talk during the time before they went to sleep. More precisely, Mary would talk, and Derrick would mostly just listen.

One evening, about ten days into their journey, as they were eating some dried meat, Derrick said, "What do you think about spending a day or two here? There are numerous deer trails throughout this area, with fresh signs scattered all around. I can get a deer and smoke it. There's a good water source, and you can spend a little time readjusting your costume."

Mary thought about it, and although she wanted to keep moving, she thought that sounded like a good idea, so she replied, "I guess that would be fine. I don't want to linger too long, but fresh meat sounds good, and I would like a break from being a fat, dirty man."

When Mary awoke the next morning, the sun was just rising. It felt good to sleep in a little, but as she looked around, she saw that Derrick was no longer there. A moment of panic flooded her heart before she noticed Derrick's bow and arrows were also missing, and it dawned on her that he was out hunting. She went to the small pond near their campsite and cleaned the dirt and grime off herself. She then returned to where they had slept and began to rework some of the straps and pouches on her clothes. She pulled out her once-white dress, which was now turning gray but was mostly clean, and put it on for the first time in weeks.

As she sat in the warmth of the sun, she was just beginning to grow drowsy when Derrick suddenly appeared out of the woods with a deer draped over his shoulders. As he made his way toward his pack, she wondered how he could move so silently in the woods. Derrick laid the deer in the grass and retrieved a rope from his pack. Mary waited to see if he would say anything, but when he didn't, she finally said, "I see you got one."

"Yes," he replied.

Mary almost sighed out loud. Derrick didn't speak much unless she drew it out of him. Sometimes when she could get him on the right topic, he would carry on a normal conversation, but soon after, he reverted to the lone woodsman. Mary said, "Well, what will you do now?"

Derrick said, "I found a good spot to make a simple smoking pit."

Mary was silent, waiting for more. She finally said, "Is that all you're going to say?"

Derrick stopped what he was doing and looked at Mary and said, "Um, I guess?"

Mary rolled her eyes, then replied, "Ok. Do you need help? No, I'm sure you don't. May I help you anyway?"

Derrick, still confused, said, "Sure." Then he picked up the deer and headed back into the woods.

Mary almost laughed as she got to her feet and followed him. Derrick slowed down a bit, so she could catch up, and hoped that waiting for her would relieve some of the tension he felt. Mary said as she caught up to him, "How long will it take to smoke the deer?"

"Until sometime tomorrow," Derrick replied.

"It's nice out, don't you think?"

"Sure"

Mary stepped in front of him and put her hands on her hips and said, "I know you can talk more than just a few words at a time; we've had conversations before. I want to talk to someone; I am tired of having to walk along beside you and not being able to speak. We're alone, talk to me."

Derrick thought they were talking, so he was a bit confused. He said, "Okay."

Mary just gaped at him, waiting. Realizing she was waiting for more, he said, "Um, what should we talk about?"

Mary did sigh out loud this time and moved out of his way as she said, "Anything you come up with. Think of a topic you will say more than three words about at a time, and that's what we'll talk about."

Derrick, feeling a bit like a trapped animal, said, "Well, you look nice, more like a girl."

Mary smiled and said, "Never mind. I'll pick the topic."

Chapter 3

Father Thomas and Odo were just leaving the chapel when Brother Jaye found them. Thomas and Odo had met with the Brothers of the Inquisition several times. They discovered little more from Odo regarding the names of any of the Templars who were involved in the worship of the mysterious Demon Baphomet. Father Thomas had noticed that the Inquisitor who had questioned the honesty of Odo's revelation about Baphomet and the Templars' involvement in a scheme to destroy Christendom was not at any of the further meetings. Thomas thought about asking what had become of the missing Brother, but decided it was probably for the best that he wasn't present any longer. Odo was suffering enough from fear of the demonic creature. The doubts of the Brother Inquisitor would only cause further confusion to Odo's already troubled mind.

Brother Jaye approached Thomas and Odo and said, "I thought I would find you two here. There has been a development that we need to discuss. Will you please accompany me?" Without waiting for a response, Brother Jaye turned and hurried back toward what Odo called the "Good Brothers' chamber." Odo and Thomas had to quicken their normally placid pace to keep Brother Jaye in sight.

As they entered the chamber, Brother Jaye quickly took his seat behind the table with the other two inquisitors. Sitting on the table in front of them was an object covered by a red cloth. As soon as Odo and Thomas entered the room, the guard closed the door from the outside. Brother Jaye, obviously excited, said, "We have been brought an item that was discovered at the commandery here in Paris. They were searching in some underground storage areas that seemed to be unused when they discovered this." As he finished speaking, he removed the red cloth, revealing a skull.

Father Thomas did not know how to react. He had expected something of greater interest than a skull. His perplexed feelings must have shown on his face because Brother Jaye continued, "I see

Father Thomas, you regard this object much as I had when it was first shown to me, but there is more. If you examine it closely, you will notice that this skull appears to be growing a beard, and that is not all."

Father Thomas was just beginning to step forward when he noticed Odo was making a high-pitched screeching noise that soon grew into a full-out scream of terror. As Thomas turned back to Odo, the squire slumped to the ground in a heap, hands covering his eyes. Thomas knelt beside him and said, "What is it, Odo? What is wrong?"

Odo appeared not to have heard him; he continued screaming. Finally, Father Thomas struck him across the face, and Odo was brought out of his fit. Father Thomas looked Odo in the eyes and repeated, "What is wrong, Odo?"

Odo pointed to the head and said, "That is the head they worship. They worship it as an idol of Baphomet."

Thomas asked, "How do you know that? You have never attended any of the secret meetings, how could you know?"

Odo looked at the head and said, "Can't you feel it? It is trying to communicate with us. It is laughing at us. Just look at it. No, don't look at it! Cover it up! Put it in a bag and drop it in the sea. Destroy it before it destroys us."

Father Thomas looked back at the skull and then at Brother Jaye, who laid the red cloth back over the skull.

Brother Jaye then said, "Odo, perhaps you could wait outside just a moment while the brothers and I discuss this matter with Father Thomas."

Odo was a bit anxious about having to leave Father Thomas, but wanting to get away from the skull, finally resolved the inner struggle and said, "Yes, I'll wait outside. Protect yourselves from that evil object."

After Odo exited the room, Father Thomas said, "He is becoming more and more separated from the world around him every day."

Brother Jaye said, "Aren't we supposed to become separated from the world around us?"

14

Father Thomas responded, "Not in the way Odo is. He has trouble grasping what is happening around him. I believe his connection with reality is slipping further away."

"Are you beginning to doubt the truth about what he is telling us regarding the Templars and their unholy worship?"

Thomas had to think quickly before he responded. When he was first brought in before the Inquisition to aid them in questioning Odo, everything had changed for the better for him. They no longer questioned his sincerity in trying to aid them against the Templars, whom he had once nominally been a member of. His treatment had drastically improved along with his prospects of a future that did not include torture and prison. If he said he doubted Odo's sanity, he might find himself being replaced. As he spent more time with the troubled young squire, he began to see the unmistakable signs of irrationality and complete refusal to recognize what was before him. After a moment, Thomas said, "No, I do not doubt Odo, but I believe that his fear of Baphomet and other minions of Hell has unhinged him, and we need to be careful what we show and say to him so that we do not add to his terrors."

Brother Jaye mollified, removed the cloth from the skull, and said, "We will keep that in mind. Now let me show you something else about this skull. The men who found it probably would never have discovered it except that, in the dark, they noticed something glowing in the corner. Brother Charles, if you will extinguish the candles."

As Brother Charles extinguished the candles in the windowless room and darkness closed in on them, Father Thomas began to see a faint green glow emanating from the skull. Brother Jaye said, "Do you see? It does not last long, but it is unmistakable. Some supernatural power has touched this totem of evil, leaving a mark. Could anyone deny that a skull that grows a beard and glows with an unholy light is of the Devil?"

Father Thomas thought the "beard" looked suspiciously like moss or lichen, and hadn't he read somewhere that some lichen glows in the dark? Again, he had to pause and consider his situation; he would not survive if he questioned or contradicted those in command of the trial against the Templars. Besides, what did he care? He was convinced the Templars were evil. What did it matter if they were convicted of worshipping a lichen-covered skull that glowed in the dark or one of the real crimes they had committed? It all leads to the same end.

As the candles were relit, Brother Jaye asked Father Thomas, "If you could speak to Odo and get any further information regarding the Templar's worship of this unholy idol, that would be of great assistance to us. We need more damning evidence if we are to convince the Papal Legate that the entire Templar organization is indeed a threat to Christendom and should be utterly expunged."

Father Thomas said, "I will speak to him immediately."

Chapter 4

Sir Henry de Creon was no longer a "Sir." He wore the robes of a novice monk and was little more than a servant among the Knights Hospitaller. When Henry was a Knight of the Temple, he never thought about all the people who did all the menial tasks at the Templar commandery. As a Templar, his focus had been on training as a knight; he only noticed the squires, novice monks, and servants when he needed them to do something for him. Now, he was one of the invisible errand boys among the Hospitallers, and it caused an almost overwhelming frustration. He was required to attend all five daily prayer services. As a knight, he could usually get out of one or occasionally two by explaining that he had an important task that could not wait. He knew many of the other Hospitaller servants enjoyed the prayer services as a time to rest, but Henry was forever restless and hated to sit still if there was anything that he felt he should do, and there was always plenty to do. Henry was assigned to muck out the stables each morning, help scour the morning breakfast utensils, split firewood, empty chamber pots, rake the practice yard during and after practice, and perform any number of other tasks anyone told him to do. Anyone whose authority was greater than his, and that included almost everyone. Worst of all, Henry could not train as a warrior. As he watched the knights, sergeants, and squires practice, he thought he might explode from not being able to get out on the sand and hold a weapon in his hands, to feel the pleasant exhaustion that came from pushing yourself hard in training.

During his first few days with the Hospitallers, he discovered about thirty previous Templars who were serving there like himself. He tried to seek them out when he could, but discovered most did not want to talk about what had happened. They were intent on keeping their heads down and remaining as inconspicuous as possible. After some searching, Henry discovered a handful who, like himself, were less content with keeping quiet about the injustice they felt they had endured. Most had been Knights or Sergeants in the Templar Order, who also had been imprisoned and tortured.

Like himself, they had all maintained their innocence of the crimes for which they were accused, so they had been allowed the opportunity to become novice monks in the Hospitallers. One day, a Father Anthony, a former priest with the Templars, was allowed to maintain his standing as a priest in the Hospitallers, yet he also felt a need to clear the name of the Templar organization.

It was Father Anthony who suggested to Henry that the group of former Templars who wished to do something should meet and decide what could be done. It was also Father Anthony who discovered a place for them to meet. The Hospitaller Commandery in Paris was not as large as that of the Templars, but there were far fewer Hospitallers stationed there than there had been Templars at the Templar commandery. The Hospitallers, perhaps because they knew a large standing army in France or England might be looked on with displeasure by the respective Kings, had decided to shift their goals after the loss of the Holy Lands. They had significantly reduced the number of members in Europe and were primarily based in Cyprus, with plans to relocate to Rhodes.

One afternoon, Father Anthony was in the sub-basement looking for candles for the chapel. While looking in the few crates scattered around the dust-filled and apparently abandoned chamber, he discovered a seemingly forgotten storage room. The entrance had been obscured by crates of forgotten items stored in the building's bowels. The room was directly below the main chapel. From the amount of dust and cobwebs, it appeared no one had been in the room for a long time. He found no candles or anything else in the sub-basement that would be of any use to anyone, but the abandoned room gave him an idea.

Father Anthony sought out Henry the next day and asked if he could help him retrieve some items from the basement. Once the two men were in the basement, Father Anthony led Henry through the trapdoor down to the sub-basement and showed him the room.

Henry looked around the forty-by-sixty-foot room by torchlight and turned to the father and said, "I don't understand. Why did you bring me here?"

Father Anthony said, "No one comes down to the sub-basement. I doubt anyone even recalls this room is here, even if they did venture below the basement level. I know that you and I both want to clear the Templar name, and there are a few other former Templars who share the same sentiment. I think we should meet and make plans. This is the perfect location. We would have to be very careful about who we include in the meetings, but I think we could do more as a group than we can do as individuals."

Henry looked around the room again, then replied, "This might work, but you are wrong on one account. I am not a 'former Templar'; I am still, and will always be, a Knight of the Temple."

Chapter 5

After spending some time watching Admiral Gregory sketch the great map in his chartbook, they all returned to Father Lull's kitchen for dinner. The cook had prepared bread stuffed with spicy pork and currants that he called "tartlets," a goose stuffed with herbs and fruit, mushrooms sautéed with leeks and ginger, and for dessert, pears colored with sandalwood and stewed in wine. It was the best meal William and Louis had ever eaten, and they both ate too much. They praised the cook lavishly, and Father Lull told them that she had once threatened to go to the Pope's court to inquire about working in his kitchens. Father Lull had lived in agony until the woman relented and said she couldn't leave the village where she was born.

After eating, Admiral Gregory tried to explain to William the significance of what the great map revealed. Father Lull decided to go for an after-dinner walk through the village, and Louis joined him. The village of Rennes-le-Château was peaceful, leaving Louis feeling welcome and safe, two emotions he hadn't experienced recently.

After walking for perhaps ten minutes, talking about the town, the pleasant weather, and the meal they had just eaten, Louis asked Father Lull, "I'd like to ask you a question, but I'm not quite sure how to ask, or even if it's appropriate."

Father Lull replied, "With an introduction like that, you must ask the question. Just ask, you don't seem the type to be overly concerned about what others think when you speak."

Louis, not sure if that was a fair comment, decided to just ask his question as best he could, "I have been a Catholic my whole life and although I've drifted here and there when it comes to being the perfect Catholic, I believe I've followed what God and the Church would have of me most of the time. I've always planned on being knighted and taking Holy Orders to become a Knight of the Temple. I've always respected the Pope as God's special servant on earth, but recently I've heard, from people I wouldn't have expected to do so, question the Church and the Pope. Now it sounds like the King and maybe the Holy See are attacking an organization I believed to be Righteous and selfless; an Order I was ready to commit my life to. It has left me confused and somewhat frightened. I feel as though everything I have based my life on has been ripped away."

Father Lull was silent for a moment and then replied in a serious tone, "Louis, my son, I am deeply sorry if my earlier comments added to your disquiet. I should have watched my tongue more closely. A common fault of mine. I have also dedicated my life to the Church, and I deeply love God, the Church as a community of believers, and the Church as an institution. Having said that, we must remember the Church is made up of men and all men are fallible. If you place your trust in any man to be perfect, you will be let down at some point, or you must choose to turn a blind eye. The Holy Roman Church is a great and massive organization. The larger an organization is, the greater the likelihood that inefficiencies and subtle deviations from the truth will occur.

"Whenever a group of people gets involved in projects with varied objectives, it is forced to make compromises, and although compromise is often good, it also often carries a seed of untruth and deception. The more objectives the group tries to accomplish, the more the seed grows. Eventually, if we are not careful, a massive tree grows from that seed, and it can overshadow the original goals of the group.

"I've often thought about writing a paper about how the practice of religion changes as the government that rules the people progresses. In a small, isolated group where there are no real leaders and the people live simply by hunting and gathering, religion is also simple. Mostly, we find that people believe in whatever they personally choose to believe. If someone trips over a stone and breaks their leg, they might decide they have offended some wandering spirit that caused the accident. As the group's size grows and they select a leader to help direct them, religion also changes. They began to believe in the spirits of the local river, trees, or the harvest, and often selected someone to be an intermediary between them and the local spirits. As they grow further and the community divides into specialties, with farmers, carpenters, bakers, and others, the community's government must also expand to coordinate everything. At this point, they usually need someone to uphold laws and perhaps lead them in times of war. The community must learn to stick together. The religion then changes to a belief in a local God that has a plan for the group of people. We see this often in the Old Testament, where we have the gods of the Canaanites, the gods of the Egyptians, and the God of the Jews. The gods in these people groups are often used to create a means of control, to encourage the populace to act in the greater good of the community, even if it may not align with their own self-interest. Then, when the population grows larger and spreads out to form multiple communities and cities/states, it reaches out to take resources from other communities. The gods and religions take on the sense that our God is the only true God, and all others are false. The idea then arises that we need to conquer those around us and utilize their resources more effectively. Consequently, we also decide it is best to convert them away from their worship of 'false gods.'

"I know this sounds cynical, and it is clearly an oversimplification of a very complex issue, but I wanted you to understand that as an organization grows, it changes. Sometimes, the changes are just to manage assets, but changes also occur because the mission evolves. With the Church, I believe, our stated mission and our actual mission have gradually grown apart at present. I believe there is too great a focus on maintaining and growing channels of power and too little focus on converting the lost, training the saints, and caring for the unprotected. I once heard a priest say that he thought every church should be dissolved after five years and then restarted with a new priest as its shepherd in a completely new building. The old church structure should be given to the homeless with everything the church possessed left in it. As impractical as that sounds, I would love to see it attempted.

"I still love the Church and its mission to teach the members and to convert the lost. I still desire, as a humble follower, to learn about and serve God in all I do, but I think it's time to shake things up a bit. I don't mean I wish to destroy or forsake, I mean to reestablish our focus. I fear that many in the clergy have lost the true meaning of Ephesians 2:8-9. They often appear to want to supplement the belief of salvation by grace with a doctrine of works."

Louis said, "Do you believe in God the same as you did before? Do you believe in the Church and the Pope the same as you did when you first became a priest?"

Father Lull said, "No, and I would not think it healthy if I did. My understanding of God has grown and changed. My original awe has evolved into something deeper and more personal, not that God is no longer full of awe, but my understanding has grown into something more profound. My faith in the Church and the Pope has also grown and waned at times. I believe the Church is a tool of God and one that has a significant influence on the mortal world, but I think we have strayed a bit, and we need to correct our course. I think the Pope is a great man, whom God has placed in the position as the leader and Spiritual guide of the Holy Catholic Church. I believe he is trying to do what is right, but I have difficulty believing everything he issues in an official Bull is the Word of God since, through Church history, too many Papal Bulls have contradicted previous ones. I understand that when tasks need to be completed by the community that are difficult, dangerous, or don't align with the views of some individuals, the leadership must have a method to motivate the populace to undertake these tasks, and the Church is often utilized in these instances. It is problematic."

Louis was about to ask another question when they heard approaching hoofbeats at a gallop. Sir Frances soon came into view as he slowed the destrier to a walk, then to a stop, and said to Father Lull in a calm tone that belied the seriousness of his words, "Father Lull, it appears we will have guests in the morning. As I was ending my circuit of the lands I was charged to guard, I noticed about fifty of the kings men camping for the night about two miles to the North of town. I would judge that about a third of their number are knights or Sergeant-at-arms; the rest appeared to be footmen and squires. I considered riding into their camp and inquiring about their intentions, but I recalled my orders from the Grand Master, which instructed me to inform you of any movement of armed men into the region before engaging in confrontations. Now that you have been informed, I will retrieve a fresh mount and ride to the hill overlooking their camp and commence confrontations on the morrow."

As Sir Frances started to wheel his horse about, Father Lull cried out, "If you could delay your return to their camp a bit, I would like for you to come back with us to the church. So that we can discuss this situation with the rest of our small company. We could use your counsel."

Sir Frances was clearly not pleased with this request, but after a moment's hesitation, he realized it could not be avoided. He replied, "I will accompany you back to the Church and report what I have seen, but I need you to understand Father, I am only bound to obey you if you have a direct command from one of my superiors, which I don't believe there is anything I am required to do for you beyond what I have already done. Regardless of what the rest of you decide to do, no one here has authority over me, and I will keep my own counsel and do what I feel is right."

Father Lull said, "I understand fully, but I do hope you will at least listen to us before you make up your mind, just as we will surely listen to you."

As Father Lull, Sir Frances, Sir William, Louis, and Admiral Gregory all sat in Father Lull's parsonage, Sir Frances recounted what he had already told Father Lull. As he finished, William asked, "Sir Frances, what do you plan on doing?"

Sir Frances said, "That all depends on them, but I do not plan on letting them enter Rennes-le-Chateau without my permission."

Admiral Gregory said, "You can't hope to stop them on your own. That is not a plan with any hope of success."

Sir Frances simply said, "That depends on how you measure success."

William said, "I will go with you, Sir Frances. Two Templars can inflict great damage to a group of untrained rabble. Maybe the sight of the two of us would be enough to turn them aside."

"I will also go. I know I'm not a knight, but I have been trained," interjected Louis.

Father Lull said, "No. This is madness. I may not be able to stop Sir Frances from getting himself killed for some misplaced idea of honor, but you two have orders from the Grand Master, and they cannot be completed if you are both dead."

Sir Frances said, "There is no such thing as misplaced honor. I believe I have done all that is required of me; I will take my leave now." And with that, the large knight left the room.

Father Lull said, after Sir Frances had left, "I thought about sending you three South to hide out in the mountains for a few days, but it's bound to be cold up there, and I think we need to get you all on your way as soon as this present crisis has passed. How do you feel about hiding in the House of God?"

Sir William was not sure if this was one of Father Lull's jokes or not, but he replied, "I'd rather not hide anywhere."

Father Lull said, "I am sure of that, but this is not yet the time to stand and fight. All you will accomplish is your own death without the opportunity to complete the orders the Grand Master has left for you."

Louis said, "I don't suppose you are ready to share those orders with us yet?"

Father Lull said, "I'm afraid not quite, but as soon as we get through the present situation, I will, I promise you. Now, if you three will follow me into the Chancel."

Father Lull led William, Louis, and Admiral Gregory to the church, where they spent several minutes placing the map sections back into their tubes. After they had gathered them, Father Lull said, "The Templars have a great secret here in Rennes-le-Château. Although I am not a Templar, I have been instructed to guard it by the Grand Master of the Order of the Templars. Not even Jon knows anything about this. I was to have revealed this to Father Thomas, and he would have taken over after me, but we will have to come up with another option. I was not instructed to tell any of you of this secret, yet under the circumstances, I believe the Grand Master would approve."

With that, Father Lull went to a flagstone on the floor near the Altar and, using a thin-bladed knife, pried it up just enough so that he could slip his fingers under and lift the stone out of the floor and reach into an open space under the stone. They all heard a 'click' near a column at the front of the church. Father Lull then went to the column and leaned his weight against it. To the astonishment of the rest of the group, the column pivoted quietly aside, revealing an opening below.

Father Lull looked at the three and said with a mischievous gleam in his eyes, "You must climb down the ladder until you reach the first landing; it is only about ten feet down. There you will find torches, flint, and steel to light them. If you will each take some of the map sections down with you, I would appreciate it."

Admiral Gregory said to William and Louis, "I'll gladly be the first down this hole. I've never been so curious in my life. What do you think a priest hides under his altar?" Then he laughed a single booming snort and slapped Louis on the back as he walked past him and started down the ladder.

Louis and William followed, and then Father Lull descended the ladder. Admiral Gregory was striking flint to steel, trying to get the torch held by Louis to catch as the father reached the small, ten-foot-by-ten-foot square landing. As the torch came to life, the men's vision extended out, and they could see they were in a large cavern. They could not tell how large, as the light only gave them faint images beyond its limited influence. Within the circle of light, they could see that steps had been cut into the stone, leading further down, and the walls extended out in all directions. They could also just make out what appeared to be bookshelves and crates neatly spaced out in the cavern below them.

"What is this place?" Sir William asked in awe.

Father Lull, with a smile, said, "This, my son, is one of the storage facilities of the Templars. It is why I am here, and it is a secret the Grand Masters and a few select individuals have kept for some time. This was built long before my arrival at Rennes-le-Château, but I have been responsible for some enhancements and alterations to maintain its secrecy. This chamber is a depository for some of the wealth of the Order. It also contains certain items that the Grand Masters have deemed worthy of special safekeeping.

"As I said earlier, Father Thomas, who the Grand Master included in your party, was to be trained as my replacement here. I guess the Grand Master misjudged the character of Father Thomas. Originally, I was not to reveal this to any of you, but I think the situation has grown beyond what the Grand Master had originally anticipated, and we are not likely to get new orders."

Louis asked, "How much money is here?"

Father Lull responded, "I have exact figures in a ledger, but let us just say 'A LOT.' There is enough just in gold and silver coin that if any Monarch had it, it would destabilize the balance of power so much that some Dynasties would likely cease to exist."

Admiral Gregory said, "You said this was 'one' of the storage facilities. Are there others?"

Father Lull said, "I may have misspoken. I have not been informed that are any other facilities like this, but I suspect there may be. The men who were occasionally sent here to work on this facility have all been Templars, and all of them were either master-masons or master-carpenters. No apprentices were allowed here. These master craftsmen were all sworn to secrecy and only spoke to me if they had specific questions regarding something they were working on. Typically, no more than two craftsmen were here at any one time, and when they finished their assigned job, they would show me what they had accomplished while here and then leave. I was never told where they went next. I always suspected that they went to other secret jobs at similar facilities.

"As for you three, we need to get a few provisions down here, some food and water, enough for a few days. You three are to hide here while the king's men are in town nosing around above. Unless by some miracle, Sir Frances can turn the king's men aside, but I doubt that is likely. He is not much for words and persuasive speech. I fear he will rely on his sword arm to speak for him."

The four of them began the task of transporting food, water, wine, and other provisions to maintain a supply for the three of them for three days. Once they felt satisfied that they had enough supplies, the good father closed the opening from above, leaving the three amongst the great wealth. It wasn't until they were secured in the underground vault that William wondered what would happen to them if something happened to Father Lull and he was unable to release them.

Father Lull then went and woke one of the men in the village who raised horses and asked him to take the horses, donkeys, and the Templars' wagon east of town and stay with them until he sent for him to return. He promised it would only be a day or two, at the most three.

Chapter 6

As the sun broke over the hills, the king's men, just rising from their night's sleep, noted a figure seated on a massive destrier atop the hill to the East. With the sun behind the lone sentinel, they had trouble making out the large banner flying from the twelve-foot pole planted into the ground beside him. After a few minutes, the sigil was clearly recognized as the Templar cross pattée, and the Knight astride his war horse also came into detail. He was covered in chain mail from the top of his head to his knees; the white Templar knight's surcoat, emblazoned with a red Templar cross, covered his torso. From the belt around his waist hung a sword on his left side and a long dagger on the right. In his right hand, he grasped a ten-foot lance; under his left arm, he held his helm. A heater shield hung from the saddle on the left side of the horse. The horse itself was also heavily armored; it wore a shining metal chamfron protecting its face. A metal peytral protected the chest of the horse, over the rest of the massive animal hung a white covering, similar to the knight's surcoat, also displaying the Templar red cross pattée on each flank.

The knight and warhorse sat silent and unmoving as the camp came to life. Orders were shouted in the camp, and the soldiers donned their armor, then began to line up in battle formation. No One knew if the single knight was alone or if, just over the hill out of sight, there might be any number of other knights Templar. They all felt his presence as a harbinger of death as they readied themselves for battle.

As the king's men started to form a line of mounted and foot soldiers, Sir Frances rode halfway to the encampment, halted, planted his lance in the ground beside him, and quietly waited. He could hear the Templar banner snapping in the morning breeze behind him, atop the hill where he left it. Three knights dressed in the King's livery approached him. As they arrived at the spot where Sir Frances waited, they came to a halt facing him. Sir Frances held up his large right hand and said, "Hail and well met. I am Sir

Frances Knight of the Temple. What brings you, good Sirs, to this humble hillside?"

At first, none of the three knights said anything. Then the one to Sir Frances' right raised his visor and spat on the ground near the hoof of Sir Frances' horse and said, "Devil worshipper."

The man in the middle also raised his visor and said, "Sir Frances, I am Lord Groombridge, and we are here at the orders of the King of France to arrest all Templars. I request that you remove your sword and surrender it to me. Then, if you would kindly climb down from your horse, kneel while my men help you remove your armor and secure you so that we may continue our journey to Rennes-le-Chateau to search out other members of your Order."

Sir Frances said, "I am afraid you gentlemen are operating under some false assumptions, but being a good Christian Knight, let me offer you some education. Firstly, as a Knight in the Holy Order of the Knights Templar, I cannot surrender 'my' sword, horse, or armor as I do not own any of those things. These items were given to me for safekeeping by my Order to further the Kingdom of God and to keep travelers safe from the various vermin that roam the land, exercising authority they do not possess. Secondly, I kneel to no man. Lastly, the good Brothers of the Knights Templar are not devil worshipers. We are men devoted to God and the Holy Cross. I will allow your party five minutes to depart from here."

Sir Groombridge said, "You know that you are just one man against fifty-seven. Unless there are others hidden over the crest of the hill behind you."

Sir Frances said, "Again, you are mistaken. I am not one man; I am an ideal. I have brothers throughout the world, and you may arrest and kill individuals here and there, but you will never conquer us. We will outlive you, your king, and your kingdom. Although some of our brothers have allowed you to arrest them and have succumbed to your torture, providing you with evidence of the lies you wish to spread about us. That time has passed. There will be no more easy surrenders; we will fight you to the death, and the final deaths of this war that you have started will be the lies you spread. You have four minutes remaining to depart."

The three riders turned and rode back to the waiting camp without another word. When they reached the line of the riders, they turned back to face Sir Frances, who still sat on his horse as they had left him. Sir Frances surveyed the twenty or so armored men on horseback with another thirty or so afoot behind them, each carrying eight-foot pikes. Scattered amongst the line, there was also a handful of crossbowmen.

Sir Frances made the sign of the cross, placed his helmet on his head, plucked his lance from the ground, grasped his shield, and raised it to protect his left side. He looked up slightly and said in a clear voice, "On behalf of God." Then he started down the hill at a gallop. Sir Frances lowered the front of the lance and couched it, then leaned slightly forward. He brought his legs back just a bit so that part of the impact of the blow could be transferred to the saddle and horse. Then he gave the horse its reins and broke into a charge.

Sir Groombridge's men were uncertain how to respond to the lone, crazy knight attacking them. As Sir Frances drew closer, they could tell he was going to attack straight into the front of their line at the extreme right wing. Before they could really do any shifting in response to the attack, the insane Templar had struck the line of knights who simply sat on their horses as if the idea of moving never occurred to them.

Sir Frances burst through the line, unseating two horsemen, one with his lance and one by bashing his shield into him. In addition, his horse trampled at least one footman and possibly more who were standing behind the mounted soldiers. Sir Frances exited the rear of the line and rode straight twenty to thirty yards, then wheeled sharply right and let the horse charge the rear of the line. The footman quickly tried to turn so that they could face the enemy who was now behind their line, but many were uncertain how to respond, and no orders were being given. Only two of the footmen raised their pikes in response to the attack from their rear, neither to any effect, as the first dropped his lance at the last minute, as he tried the leap to the side as the frothing horse drew down on him. The other footman was shaking too much to seat the back of the pike in the ground or to properly angle and aim at the horse's chest. Both

31

were ridden down and killed beneath thundering hooves. The horsemen had only partly completed their turn when Sir Frances struck through the rear of their line. One more was unhorsed by Sir Frances's lance, which snapped off in the man's side.

Again, Sir Frances rode past the line, wheeled left this time, threw his broken lance to the side, drew his sword, and continued the attack without halting. This time, the mounted soldiers were ready for the charge and put up resistance, but being committed to the line of defense, they stood little chance against the brave knight who seemed to be single-handedly dismantling their defense. On this pass, he slew one mounted soldier with his sword and crushed more footmen with his horse. When he slowed to wheel right again, a crossbow bolt glanced off his helmet, and another buried itself in his leg. He took no notice and continued his attack without slowing.

Lord Groombridge may have been slow to appreciate the seriousness of this lone attacker, but after four passes through his line, he ordered his men to wheel to the right and fan out to attack the Templar from the side. He also ordered all the crossbowmen to open up on him as he wheeled his horse. This maneuver was carried out in a ragged manner. During this time, Sir Frances was able to make two more passes through the line, with a similar effect, before Lord Groombridge's men could shift to the offense.

As Sir Frances went through the line the sixth time, he had two riders approaching from his left at a gallop and several more behind them. He turned to face the attack and once again gave his horse its reins as two crossbow bolts struck the horse, one in the neck and the other in its chest just above the peytral. The great destrier's front legs gave out, and Sir Frances found himself going headfirst over the front of the horse, losing his sword in the fall. He rolled forward and managed to come to a halt on his knees as one of the mounted soldiers leaned to the side and tried to drive his sword through the kneeling knight. He grabbed the man's wrist and upper arm as the blade buried itself several inches into Sir Frances' shoulder. Sir Frances hung onto the man's arm and dragged him from the saddle. As the king's men crashed to the ground, Sir Frances drew the knight's sword from his own shoulder and stood to meet the next rider. He made a spoiling sweep with the sword that deflected the lance that would have pierced his midsection, but as he shifted his weight to meet the next rider, his leg with the crossbow bolt in it gave out, and he stumbled directly into the path of the man's horse. One of the sharp hooves came down full on his chest, and he heard bones breaking. Another caught him just above the groin, and a third kicked him hard just under his chin, breaking his jaw and knocking out most of his teeth. The straps that held his helmet in place also snapped, the helmet came free, and rolled across the field of battle. He was still conscious when Lord Groombridge rode up and dismounted beside him.

Lord Groombridge looked down on the broken man spread out before him. With no little amount of respect, and said, "Sir Knight. I have never seen an act so brave and well-executed in my many years of campaigning."

Sir Frances said through smashed teeth, "I learned my stitching from Sergeant Bertrand; he taught me well."

Lord Groombridge, not understanding the reference to sewing, supposed the man's wits had been scrambled and chose to ignore the comment. He knelt beside Sir Frances and said quietly, "I wish I did not have to do this, but I see no other option." He drew his long dagger and drove it quickly into Sir France's left eye and into his brain.

Lord Groombridge then wiped the blade on the Templar's surcoat and said to one of his mounted soldiers nearby, "Leave a few men here to care for the wounded and bury the dead. The rest of us leave for Rennes-le-Chateau immediately.

Chapter 7

Mary sliced the deer meat into thin strips as Derrick had instructed her. While she did that, Derrick dug a four-foot-deep pit in the ground and started a fire at the bottom of the pit. He kept adding hardwood logs to the pit until he had a thick bed of charred wood and ash in the bottom, then he layered a few large flat stones on the red-hot embers. Then, a loose layer of branches he had soaked in the nearby stream. On top of this, he and Mary laid out the meat, then another layer of soaked branches, more meat, and so on, until it was finally covered with a layer of thicker branches. After they had finished, Derrick sat down and started to clean and sharpen his knife.

Mary sat next to him and said, "Now what?"

Derrick responded, "We wait."

Mary continued to look at him for a moment and finally said, "Until…?"

Derrick stopped sharpening his knife and said, "In the morning, the meat will be dried, and we can pack up and go."

Mary said, "I'll go get my costume and make some adjustments in a minute. Right now, I just want to sit here." After a pause, Mary continued, "You know you've never really asked me about why I want to go to Rennes-le-Château."

Derrick said, "You have indicated that you had friends there."

Mary replied, "Well, not really friends. I was traveling with a group of Knights Templar to Rennes-le-Château, and we were attacked in the town of Vézelay when the king's men attempted to arrest the Templars. We weren't too far out of Paris, so they decided to send part of the group back to Paris to discover what was going on. I accompanied the group that returned to Paris. When we approached the Templar commandery, things got chaotic, and the Templars I was with were taken by the king's men. Odo, a squire in our group, told me to ride away, and, in all the confusion, I alone was able to escape. I feel that I need to inform the other group about what happened to their comrades, but I fear that this will all be a waste of time. They may already have arrived in Rennes-le-Chateau and possibly moved on, or worse, they could have also been arrested.

Derrick thought for a moment, then said, "Why is the King arresting Templars? I thought they were knights of the Church or something?"

Mary said, "I don't really know, the people who tried to arrest them in Vezelay called them heretics and other evil things. One man, I recall, shouted that they were in league with the Muslims. It was all very unsettling and happened very fast. One of the Templars, the one known as Bertrand, was skilled and formidable in battle. He was a little frightening even when he was sitting silently on his horse. The whole situation is strange, and I don't know why I feel compelled to try and reach the others. I also feel bad for involving you in this mess. Yet any time I consider stopping and just getting on with my life, I feel a pang of overwhelming guilt."

Derrick said, "I've never met a Templar. Could the accusations of evil against them by the people of Vezelay be true? I did know a man from Vezelay. I traded with him to obtain high-quality yew wood, which I used to make my bows. He seemed to be an upright man, not one I'd suppose would attempt to attack honest people."

Mary stood and said with her hands on her hips, "NO! The Templars are good men; they saved me and protected me. I know they are good, God-fearing men! I'm going to get my garb now."

As she stormed away, Derrick thought to himself, 'I believe I saved and protected you, too.' Then he took a leather strap out and began to strop the knife's edge.

The rest of the afternoon was spent with Mary reworking her costume and Derrick hunting down a Rabbit and a quail, which they ate that day and the next morning before continuing their journey.

Mary and Derrick traveled another two weeks along the road without incident. For a couple of days, they rode in the back of a wagon that a merchant was using to haul some empty wine casks to Marseille. They could have ridden nearly all the way to the coast, but Mary, having to pretend she was mute the whole time, couldn't bear not being able to at least talk freely to Derrick in the evening hours, so they parted company with the merchant.

They reached the outskirts of Avignon near dark. They decided to make camp outside the city and enter in the morning. The plan was to purchase a few supplies and ask about which road to take next and how much further it was to Rennes-le-Chateau.

That next morning, they entered the town. There was an air of excitement in the town, and the people were eagerly exchanging bits of gossip with anyone who would listen. Two Cardinals from King Philip had arrived the day before, and there were many rumors about the war of words between the King and the Pope, regarding the Templars.

While gathering supplies and information regarding the last leg of their trip, they also discovered information regarding the Templars. It seemed that at first, the Pope was incensed that King Philip had arrested the Templars. However, as confessions began to emerge, Pope Clement V changed his mind and even indicated that he had known about the accusations against the Templars years before, but he had simply not believed them. Following these confessions, the Pope felt he had no choice but to issue a papal decree, ordering the other Monarchs of the Latin kingdoms to arrest the Templars in their lands and seize all their properties, holdings, and possessions in the name of the Pope.

Then, just the day before Derrick and Mary arrived, the Pope had discovered that King Philip IV had no intention of releasing any of his prisoners to the Church. It appeared King Philip planned to maintain possession of all lands and possessions he had confiscated from the Templars when he made his move back in October. The Pope was enraged. Those lands had been donated to the Templars as a gift to God; the King had no right to them. All that the Templars owned and controlled clearly belonged to the Church. Everyone was waiting for word of what the Pope would do next.

They also heard many rumors about the Templars. That the Grand Master had himself confessed to devil worship, homosexuality, and defecating on the cross. As they made their way out of the town, Mary was visibly angry, and Derrick was afraid she

36

might verbally attack some of those making accusations against the Templars, but she held her tongue and maintained her role of a mute fat man. They had traveled less than a mile from Avignon before Mary quietly told Derrick she wanted to go into the woods and talk. They moved a few hundred feet into a thick stand of poplar trees, and Mary began to talk in what started as a hushed voice but soon grew louder. Mary said, "Can you believe those people? They actually believe the Templars did all those evil things. A few months ago, it would have been insane to accuse them of these things, but now they talk like everyone has always known the Templars were conspiring with evil. It just makes me so…mad." At this point, her shoulders dropped, and her hands went to her face as she began to sob.

Derrick, without hesitation, enfolded her in his arms. The act shocked Mary almost as much as it did Derrick. As Mary cried into his chest, Derrick had no idea how this hug was supposed to end. He felt a strong urge to release her and perhaps pat her on the back until she stopped crying, but he didn't seem to be able to make his arms loosen from her padded form. As Mary's sobbing turned to shudders and she regained control of herself, she looked up at Derrick with the dirt and soot streaking her cheeks, she said in a pleading tone, "You don't think it's true, do you? I mean, even the Pope seems to think they are guilty. Could I have misjudged them? Are they working with demons? Are the Templars truly evil?"

Derrick was silent for a moment, trying to gather his thoughts; he finally said, "I have no real feelings about or experience with the Church or the Knights Templar. I have had interactions with the King's men, and I do not trust them. From what you've said, the Templars were once respected knights and representatives of the Church, but then they were suddenly considered evil. It seems that the accusations they are facing have been ongoing for some time in secret, and now that they have suddenly come to light, everyone appears to be convinced that they are true. I find it strange that this would just become evident overnight. Before a tree falls over, rotten and decayed, there are signs of its impending demise. Leaves turn brown before Fall and don't grow back in Spring; branches fall off, first small ones, then large ones. I think it would be the same with an organization as large as the Templars. There should have been many signs of the evil that would become increasingly obvious for some time before they are suddenly found to be in league with Satan. It seems more likely someone wants revenge or desires their lands and possessions. I find it easier to believe the Templars are in the way of someone or some idea more powerful and are being set up for some reason."

Mary released her hug and looked up at Derrick, then she kissed him on the lips for a long moment. Derrick tasted the salty tears as her lips pressed against his. He was lost in conflicting feelings and was just beginning to relax as Mary ended the kiss. "You never cease to amaze me. How someone who has spent so much time away from people has such great knowledge of them makes no sense to me."

After a moment, Derrick said a little flushed, "I never thought my first real kiss would be from a dirty, fat man who needs a haircut."

Chapter 8

It was late at night; nearly everyone was asleep. Father Thomas had spent most of the day with Odo trying to discover more about the skull he claimed was an idol of Baphomet, but Odo refused to talk about it other than to say that it needed to be destroyed. Father Thomas knew that Brother Jaye wanted more information and was growing impatient with Odo. They were supposed to meet with Father Jaye and his brother Inquisitionists in the morning, and so far, he had nothing to add. He said in a mild tone, hoping to get Odo to cooperate, "Odo, please, the good Brothers of the Inquisition need more information. You said the skull was an idol they worshipped; how do you know that? Have you seen it before, or has someone told you about it?"

Odo stared at the ground and seemed not to have heard Father Thomas. Thomas noticed that his breathing was slow and regular, so he was not about to go into a manic fit, as he had on previous occasions when discussing topics that upset him. Father Thomas took that for a good sign and decided to press a little more, "Did you see the head in a vision? Is that how you know that the Templars worshipped it?" Again, he paused, and Odo still just sat there with his head bowed.

As Father Thomas was about to try again, Odo said softly in a voice that sounded more like the old Odo before his arrest, "Father, I'm so confused. I feel as though I have two voices in my head, one being me and the other something else. This 'other' is bent on seeing the Templars destroyed. The other voice has more control most of the time, and I can't seem to stop him from saying things I do not believe are true. When I try to speak to him, he shouts and screams and cries and will not listen. I'm not sure where that voice is right now; it's as if he has gone to sleep, and I can finally think and speak without his ravings drowning me out. Father, I know you are trying to help, but I can't tell you anything about that skull; the other might claim to know something, but they are mad. I'm afraid that soon I will be mad too."

Father Thomas did not know what to say or do. A few times, there had been brief glimpses of the old Odo, but nothing like this. It terrified Thomas. The manic Odo was the one he needed; if Odo was of no use to the Inquisition, then Father Thomas was of no use. Thomas said, "Odo, my son, I'm sure this is all very exhausting, and you need a break. Perhaps after we have delved a little deeper into the worship of the skull, you and I can take a break and leave this place for a while."

Odo looked up and interrupted Thomas, "You don't understand. That other voice is false; he lies, and nothing he says can be trusted. I don't recall ever hearing the word Baphomet before I heard it come out of my own mouth. I was locked in that room with other Templar squires and functionaries, and after a few days, I tried to escape. I couldn't take being in there any longer, but when I tried, I was hit on the head by a guard, and after that, this other voice started. At first, I could barely hear it in the back of my head. It was like the buzzing sound an insect makes, but it grew louder and louder. Then the buzzing became words, crazy words. The crazy words began to become shouts, and I couldn't make the crazy voice quiet enough to hear me. The other voice took over." At this point, Odo became a little frantic; he seized the father's hands. Odo looked into Thomas's eyes, and Thomas noticed the distant, haunted look that he had seen in Odo's eyes was gone, and replacing it was a pleading, pained look.

Odo continued, "Father, you must help me. I don't want to do or say anything that can further the attack on my brother Templars, but I don't know if I can stop the other voice. He's quiet now, as though the fear of that skull has driven him into hiding. He is terrified of the skull more than anything else, but he won't stay there long; he will be back. I can't take it. You must help me stop the other voice. You were a Templar; you know there was no devil worship or other evils they accuse us of. It's all false, brought on by lies and hysteria. While the voice is quiet, you must help me reveal the truth to the Inquisition.

Father Thomas nearly struck Odo. He needed the other Odo back, not this one! This Odo was going to get himself burned at the stake as a relapsed heretic, and Thomas returned to a cell awaiting torture and/or death. Father Thomas was a calculating man; he knew it would be of no use to physically or verbally attack Odo. He also didn't believe Odo could be convinced to continue the story that the 'other voice' had begun. He feared that even if the 'other voice' returned to prominence, there was no way to guarantee that the old Odo would not reappear again at the wrong moment. So, Father Thomas knew that he and Odo had to escape the situation they were in, even though it meant great risk to them both.

Father Thomas said, "Odo, we must leave this place at once. I believe we can leave now if we go at once, while most of the castle is asleep. We will have to inform any guards we encounter that we are on a mission for the Inquisition that cannot be delayed. Leave the talking to me."

Odo looked confused. "But if we leave, we can't tell the Inquisition the truth."

Thomas said, "That is correct, but if we just go in there tomorrow and tell them the truth, they will not believe us and will just silence both of us. Besides, in the morning, your 'other voice' might have awoken and regained control, then where would we be?"

Odo said, "You could tell them the truth and explain the other voice."

Father Thomas replied, "Would that I could. They would not believe me; they are already convinced of what you have already said. We must leave, escape this place. We will find other Templars committed to getting the truth out in a way that will be effective in clearing the damage your confessions have caused."

Odo looked stricken by shame and replied softly, "You are right, Father."

Thomas said, "Good. Now follow me. We can take nothing but the clothes on our backs. Just stay beside me and don't say a word to anyone. I will handle it all."

They left the room and entered the main hall. They made their way to one of the towers and began climbing the steps. After climbing most of the way up the tower, Odo said in a whisper,

41

"Father Thomas, where are we going? Shouldn't we be heading for the front gates, not going up?"

Father Thomas also said, in a whisper, "No, we will exit the tower onto the top of the wall and go along the parapet until we reach the tower going down to the postern gate; there is a sally port there that I hope we might leave by unnoticed. Now, please remain quiet."

They exited the Tower onto the battlement on the top of the castle wall. Father Thomas started walking at a brisk pace. The wind was blowing, and the night was chilly as their robes whipped around them. As they were about to enter another tower, Father Thomas stopped and asked Odo, "Did you hear that?"

Odo listened a moment and said quietly, "No, I didn't hear anything."

Thomas leaned through an embrasure and looked at the ground some sixty feet below. When he straightened back, he whispered to Odo, "You have a look, my eyes aren't as good as yours."

As Odo leaned out to look down, along the base of the wall, Father Thomas shoved him from behind. Odo, as he began to lose his balance, twisted sideways and grabbed hold of Thomas' sleeve. Thomas and Odo's eyes locked together. Thomas said in a strained whisper, "Odo, don't you see this is the only way to keep the Order safe? With you alive and that 'other voice' shouting lies that will discredit the Templars, you will always be a threat to honesty. Once you are gone, I can tell the inquisition the truth, and that other voice will not be around to contradict me. I know suicide is a mortal sin, but this is not suicide; that is why I tricked you into coming up here. The sin will not be on your soul."

Odo's look of terror slowly faded to confusion, then even more slowly to comprehension and peace. He said, "I understand, Father. Please do all you can to correct the evil I have caused. I trust in you, Father. I know you will do what is right." Then he released his grip and toppled backward from the wall.

Chapter 9

Henry had spoken with three former Templar knights about meeting together after midnight to discuss the idea of trying to clear the Templars' name, and he knew that Father Anthony had spoken to four other former Templars. As Henry made his way quietly to the sub-basement, he saw up ahead of him that there were already some men present in the room. He moved as quietly as possible and was able to get outside the meeting room without being noticed. He stood quietly beside the door and listened. There were at least three voices, and he recognized one, Peter, previously Sir Peter de Rhone. The three men were speaking of the way they were being treated as servants when they were rightful members of the Chivalry. They also spoke about how they would make the Knights Hospitaller, who had treated them so poorly, apologize or face them on the field of honor as soon as they had righted this mistake being perpetrated against their Order.

Henry noticed a figure quietly making its way toward the room, and as the ghostlike shape drew closer, he recognized it as Father Anthony. As Father Anthony was about to enter the door, Henry cleared his voice softly. The Father, not noticing Henry beside the door, was slightly startled. Henry said, "Forgive me, Father, I thought clearing my voice would be less surprising than just stepping out of the blackness."

Father Anthony replied, "That's quite all right. Why were you hiding in the shadows in the first place?"

Henry said, "I was listening to our compatriots in there. We will need to establish some security protocols for these meetings and establish rules regarding what we say to each other. Otherwise, we will find ourselves back under lock and key and will be of no use to anyone. Let's go on in, and as soon as the others arrive, we should get the meeting started. I think our first order of business must be clarification on how sensitive and secretive our situation truly is, and that our goals should be for the greater good of the Templars as an Order, not us as individuals."

Henry took charge of the meeting as the ninth and last person arrived. "Gentlemen, I am thankful that all of you have come. And I am relieved that, as Father Anthony and I have spoken to you, we have discovered we were not alone in our desire to expose the lies that are being told about our Order. We are all Templars; we have among us seven knights: Peter de Rhone, Gabriel du Breze, Louis d'Aubigne, Victor de Lorraine, Jules de Verneuil, Gaspard de Troyes, and I, Henry de Creon; one priest, Father Anthony; and one master stonemason, Master Jamison. Before we can discuss how to rectify the terrible wrongs that have been committed against us Templars, we must first ensure that we can converse and plan in complete secrecy. I propose, as a first measure, that we post a guard with sword drawn outside the door, just as was done in past meetings of Templar knights. Secondly, we refrain from discussing anything we have discussed in these meetings outside of this room. I don't believe I need to tell you how dangerous it would be for all of us if just one of us were to slip up. I'm sure there are other former brothers out there who would gladly join our cause, but we must be very careful about who we approach and allow to join.

"I believe all members of our group should have to make a formal oath before God that speaks of our intentions and swears on pain of death not to reveal anything about what we do here or who has attended the meetings. Father Anthony, would you please come up with an appropriate oath that we will all take at our next meeting?"

Father Anthony said, "I would be happy to. May I add that I think we must all agree to admit anyone new before anyone approaches a potential new member?"

Henry replied, "Yes, I agree that would be a good idea. What do you think, brothers?" All the former Templars gave their consent.

Henry continued, "I want to say at the outset that my intention in meeting together here is not just to have fellowship with fellow former Templars. I consider myself to still be a Templar, and I am still willing to lay down my life for God, the Church, and the Order. I am aware that the Church is involved in these accusations against the Order, which have raised some concerns for me. I have made a vow, and although in the past, I may have ruffled at some of The Rule and what I saw as a lack of initiative on the part of the Templar hierarchy, I will do all in my power to defend and restore the good name of the Templars. Whoever is responsible for this travesty will pay, or I will die trying. That is my intent; if you disagree, I will leave and continue on my own.

The other eight men looked around at each other and, without a word, as one came to an agreement, gave their assent. Jamison, the mason, said for them all, "I believe we are all in agreement, and I, for one, will approach this great endeavor with the same commitment and attention to detail as I would the construction of a great cathedral."

Henry, relieved to hear their agreement, said, "As to the organization of these gatherings, I have taken the lead here, but that is just because someone has to, and Father Anthony and I organized this first meeting. How should we establish who directs our discussions and assigns tasks?"

Chapter 10

The king's men, led by Lord Groombridge, rode up to Rennes-le-Chateau just before the noon hour. The small town was quiet, and one might have thought it abandoned were it not for the fresh laundry hanging on the lines and the Priest that stood before the church. Lord Groombridge, who still had the blood of Sir Frances splattered on his armor, said, "Father, I am Lord Groombridge, and we have been sent by King Philip to apprehend three Templars who have been sent here by their former Grand Master and confiscate property that belongs to the Crown of France."

Father Lull said with a smile on his face, "The only Templar I know of rode off last night with the intention of, how did he put it? Ah yes, 'engaging in confrontations' with you gentlemen."

Lord Groombridge said, "Sir Frances was indeed very…confrontational. I am truly sorry to say that that brave man is now dead. I would prefer not to have to kill any others, but I have orders from my Lord King, and I must carry them out. Now, about these other three Templars, unless Sir Frances was one of the three we were sent here for, in which case, it would be the other two Templars. If you would kindly tell me where they are, we will collect them and the King's Property and leave your beautiful little town."

Father Lull said, "Although it pains me to hear that Sir Frances has been killed, I know that he died in the manner of his own choosing. I am in no hurry to see you gentlemen depart. I enjoy conversations with strangers."

Lord Groombridge waited a few moments to see if the father would say anything about the other Templars and then signed, "I am truly sorry, Father, but I cannot leave without the men and property I was sent here to retrieve." Then he yelled to his men, who had all remained in their saddles during the conversation, "Dismount and search the entire town."

There was a sudden commotion as the twenty-odd soldiers began to dismount and disperse into the town. But then a voice halted them.

From the main entryway of the church, Jon shouted, "There is no need for that, Lord Groombridge. The men and the objects you seek, and much more, are here within this Church."

Father Lull was caught as much by surprise as the rest of the men. They all turned to look at Jon as Father Lull said, "Jon, have you been in the sacramental wine? What are you talking about?"

Jon, with the first expression of anger Father Lull had ever seen on his face, said, "I am talking about a priest who is lying to a Lord in the lawful service of his King. I am talking about a priest who has allied himself with a group of ungodly Templars and is hiding secrets from the devout people of this country. I am talking about a priest who allows known Cathers to congregate in clandestine meetings in the woods around here. I am talking about you, Father Lull."

Lord Groombridge said in a commanding voice to his men, "You five, come with me. The rest of you continue your search of the town. Father, I believe I would like you to accompany me also."

As they entered the Church, Jon said, "Father Lull has been dealing with Templars since before I came here a few years ago. There always seems to be a Templar knight or two here just roaming around the countryside. Father Lull has them keep their horses in the Church stable, and the knights usually reside in the guest room while here. What is truly odd, though, is that sometimes a craftsman or two arrives, remains here for a few weeks or months, and then departs. I never see them working anywhere. I may see them very early in the morning or late at night, but I never see them during the day, and there are no noticeable changes anywhere in the church or even in the entire village. So, I started watching when a craftsman arrived; on several occasions, I would see them in the church, and then they would disappear without ever leaving the building. I know there is a secret place here in this building."

Lord Groombridge looked from Jon to Father Lull, who simply shrugged as if he had no idea what Jon was on about. Lord

Groombridge then said to Jon, "Do you know where the secret hiding place is?"

Jon replied somewhat sheepishly, "No, my Lord, but it is in this building, I'm certain of it. Just ask him."

Lord Groombridge said to Father Lull, "Father, I don't suppose you care to make this easy and tell me where the secret hiding place is?"

Father Lull held his hands out at his side, palms up, and said, "Lord Groombridge, I'm afraid I have no idea what Jon is talking about. Yes, Knight Templars do occasionally stay here, and they do seem to feel this town is under their protection, but the rest of what Jon said baffles me as much as you. This is the House of God, not a castle with secret passageways and hidden rooms. Jon has never shown any indication of insanity in the past, so I can only imagine he has mistaken things he supposes he has seen."

Lord Groombridge, while looking at Father Lull, said to his men, "Start searching the Church, but keep in mind what this building is and try not to damage or desecrate anything. Father, if you will accompany Jon and me on the Chancel, we three will look up there."

As Lord Groombridge and Jon thumped on walls and stomped on the floor, Father Lull looked on patiently, seemingly amused. Lord Groombridge said to him, "So, you knew Sir Frances. How did that friendship develop?"

Father Lull said, "I'm afraid 'friend' would not be the correct description of our relationship. Sir Frances arrived one day a few months back and 'requested' to keep his horses in our stables and food and shelter for himself while he was here. I know that sounds a little presumptuous, but I have been the priest here for over six years, and as Jon said, there seems to always be a Templar knight or two here. I was informed it has been that way since long before my arrival."

Lord Groombridge took a break from tapping on walls and looked at Father Lull, saying, "And what were the Templars doing here?

Father Lull shrugged and said, "I really don't know. They would eat and pray here, but mostly they roamed around the countryside. I asked a few of them at first why and always got some version of the same answer. They would say something like, 'We are trained to always be vigilant.' Or 'Even if this is not the Holy Lands, Templars are sworn to protect travelers.' Or 'I cannot merely sit around and pray all day.' It always seemed to me they were looking for something or someone. As time went on, I just assumed it was either part of their training or possibly that the knights who were sent here were being punished for some infraction of their Rule. I am sorry, but I really don't know what they were doing here."

Lord Groombridge said, "It sure seemed to me that Sir Frances was doing more than looking. He appeared to be very adamant that we not enter this town. I believe he was protecting something or someone...or both."

Father Lull said, "I cannot say, as I mentioned, we were not close. Some of the Templars who spent time here were more talkative than others, and some seemed to desire to keep to themselves more than others, but none have been as disinclined to interact with me or anyone else in the village as Sir Frances. I believe the longest conversation I had with him was last night before he rode out to meet you, gentlemen."

Lord Groombridge asked, "I don't suppose you would tell me what that conversation was about?"

Father Lull shrugged and said, "I have no problem telling you. He told me of your arrival and said he was going to engage you, gentlemen, in a confrontation. When I tried to talk him out of it and indicated I did not understand why he felt that any confrontation was necessary, he said I had no authority over him and left. As I told you, he was a man of few words."

Lord Groombridge looked at Father Lull for a brief second as if he expected more, then resumed his probing for the hidden room.

After searching for over an hour and finding nothing that would indicate a false wall or trap door or anything out of the ordinary, Lord Groombridge said to Jon, "I am not sure how to look any further without tearing walls down or ripping up the floor, which I am not going to do to a Church. Do you have any additional information that would indicate the location of the secret place? Or any proof that what you say is true. If not, I think we must continue our search of the rest of the town."

Jon, who had at first scampered with great energy all over the front of the Church, had fallen into a silent sulk as they came up with nothing. Finally, he said, "I know it's here somewhere. I know he's hiding them. One man has been here for several weeks. I don't know if he's a Templar, but I know he drinks and has the arrogance of one. And two other men arrived yesterday with a wagon; they had some scrolls of paper that they assembled into a large map in this very room just last night. Although they seemed much less arrogant than Templars I've previously met, I'm sure they are."

Lord Groombridge said, "You mean to tell me you do not even know if these men you saw were Templars? You also say that the object they transported was a map?! Do you think it is possible that these two men, who arrived yesterday, simply came here to ask for Father Lull's guidance, and they showed him a map to help them get to where they were going? Could these men have just left Rennes-le-Chateau early this morning while you were busy elsewhere?"

Jon, somewhat shaken, said, "No, that is not right. They had me watch the wagon like they were concerned its contents might be taken. The map was no ordinary map; it was locked up and was very large. And this Priest also does nothing to stop the heretical Cathers from meeting and spreading their evil Gnostic theology around here. He must be stopped. Take him to the Inquisition; they will get the truth. This man cannot be allowed to shepherd the people of this town." As he spoke, his voice grew louder and sharper until the last words were little more than a shriek.

Lord Groombridge clenched his fists and said, "I don't give a damn about any Cathers! Is that what this is about? Are you so worked up over a few Cathers that you accuse this man of God?"

Lord Groombridge said to Father Lull, "I am sorry, Father. I think you had best attend to your man here. I would advise removing him from this community; he clearly has something against you, and his imagination has gotten the better of him. If you like, I can have my men take him into custody, and we can take him to Toulouse with us when we leave here."

Father Lull said, "Thank you, Lord Groombridge, but I don't believe that is necessary. Maybe I have overworked poor Jon. He is clearly distraught. I will send him to his chamber for the rest of the day to spend it in quiet prayer and thought. In the morning, we will talk about appropriate penance. And perhaps he is correct, I have been rather lenient with the few Cathers that remain here, but I do not think they truly pose a threat to the True Faith."

Then Father Lull said to Jon, "Jon, if you will kindly go to your chamber and do as I have asked."

Jon was about to argue when he saw Lord Groombridge place a hand on the hilt of his sword, and he knew he could do nothing else…here…and now. As he made his way to his chamber, he said under his breath, "You have not won yet, Father Lull."

After Jon had left the Church proper, Lord Groombridge said to his men, "You men, go out and help search the rest of the town, but be respectful of the citizens here."

As they left, he added to the father, "Now, Father Lull, I still have a job to perform. Jon spoke of two men with a map. Could they have been Templars in disguise?"

Father Lull rubbed his chin a moment and said, "Well, I don't really think so. They arrived yesterday, as Jon said, but they wore no Templar garb, and they were both clean-shaven. I've never met a Templar without a beard. They said they were on their way to Bayonne, where they hoped to find work at the docks. They stopped here to ensure they were on the right road, and I offered a safe place to rest and a meal in exchange for conversation, which I hold in high value. As you had said, they departed this morning just as the sun rose."

Lord Groombridge said, "You're probably right, but all the same, I will have to consider the possibility. The Templars we are looking for were supposed to be heading to this town. Have you seen any other men pass through here recently? There are supposed to be three with a wagon."

"Just those two." Father Lull replied. "It's a quiet town if anyone else had arrived here. I'm sure I would have known. Do you suppose Rennes-le-Chateau is just a way station on the way to the mountains to the South? I've often wondered if it was something of that nature that might explain why the Templars were roaming the countryside. Maybe Sir Frances met the men you are seeking and guided them around the town to head into the mountains. Many travelers use the mountain passes as a way into Spain when they want to do so secretly."

Just then, one of Lord Groombridge's men entered the Church and said, "Begging your pardon, my Lord, but we have completed the search of the town, and there is nothing here."

Lord Groombridge said, "Very well. Have the men mount up; we will be leaving shortly."

Lord Groombridge sighed and said, "I really hate this. I have always considered myself a man of honor and duty, so when I received orders from the King to find these Templars, I committed myself to do what I must. I have heard all the stories about the Templars that are being spread throughout France, yet I have known many Templars and have a hard time reconciling what is being said with the men I have known.

"I have no orders to travel into Spain, so if that is what happened with the men I seek, they are lost to me. I suppose I need to head West to Bayonne and seek the two men who were here; that appears to be my best lead. After our confrontations with Sir Frances, I have families back home who I will have to make accommodations for."

Father Lull said, "Would you and your men care to stay the night here? I should be able to find billets for your men in town, and we can provide you with a good meal to set you on your way in the morning.

Lord Groombridge replied, "Thank you, Father, but no. I still have men North of town I need to gather before we head West, and I'd like to meet these two men before they reach Bayonne and disappear into the wharf area. Many men come and go through there every day."

As Lord Groombridge was about to exit the Church, he said, as if to himself, but loud enough for Father Lull to hear him clearly, "I believe if I were a Templar, whether I was a knight or a cowherd or even a kind priest who had dealings with Templars, I would board a ship and depart France to make a new home beyond the reach of both King and Pope."

Chapter 11

It took about another week of walking for Mary and Derrick to reach Rennes-le-Chateau from Avignon. They met very few people on their way, although one encounter left them somewhat puzzled. About three days out from Rennes-le-Chateau, they met a man in the robes of a monk or priest headed in the direction they had come from. He said his name was Jon and that he was going to see the Pope in Avignon. He asked where they were headed, and when Derrick told him Rennes-le-Chateau, he grew instantly agitated. He began to carry on about a priest who beguiles his congregation into thinking he is a man of God when he is truly a servant of Hell. He ranted on regarding how he conspires with Cathers and Templars and keeps dark secrets from the Church. By the time Jon had finished his tirade, he was nearly frothing at the mouth and seemed to have forgotten that he had been speaking to them as he suddenly continued his walk heading East, still carrying on about the evils of the Cathers.

Later that day, after meeting Jon, Mary decided she had had enough of her disguise and disappeared into the woods to change into her regular clothes and bundle up the costume. She felt much lighter and freer, finally unencumbered by the padding and straps. And she was truly relieved to be able to talk to Derrick whenever she chose.

When Mary and Derrick walked into the quiet village of Rennes-le-Château, it was late afternoon. As they were seated near a well, trying to decide whom to approach and how to ask about Mary's friends who might have arrived, they noticed a priest walking toward them. They wondered if this was the father, the crazy man Jon had spoken of. The priest approached them and, with a broad, easy smile, said, "Hello, I am Father Lull. What brings you to our beautiful town?"

Mary said, "Hello, Father. My name is Mary, and this is Derrick. We have come here to meet some friends who were supposed to have arrived ahead of us. Three men, they would have arrived with several horses and a wagon."

Father Lull looked at them searchingly for a moment, then smiling even more broadly, said, "Mary, I am very pleased to meet you. I don't recall anyone mentioning someone named Derrick, but I am pleased to meet you both. I'm afraid you missed your friends by just a couple of days, but I am eager to hear your story and share what I can regarding our mutual friends. I am off to get food. If you would like to walk with me, we can talk some, and after that little errand, we can return to the church where we can eat an evening meal while we continue to get to know each other."

They walked along the stone-paved road to one of Father Lull's parishioners, where they collected some fresh vegetables, sliced and soaked in oil and vinegar, and a pot with freshly prepared chicken in a white sauce that smelled heavenly. The lady who gave the basket of food to Father Lull was pleasant enough, but she gave both Mary and Derrick a look filled with suspicion. The woman accepted a hug from Father Lull as thanks for the food, and while the good Father wasn't looking, she looked directly at Mary and gave the sign of the evil eye, then spat on the ground before vanishing into her house.

As they started on their way to the Church, Father Lull chuckled and said, "You must forgive Patricia. She is always kind and helpful, but as she has aged, she has grown weary of strangers and is not very appreciative of change. She has six sisters, and they all live here in this little village. They are all a delight and a trial to me.

"Let me see. There is Violet. She is the oldest and is always welcoming and willing to help, especially if she senses injustice being done to others who cannot defend themselves. The more difficult the situation is, the more energy she will invest in resolving it. I can often see the wheels turning behind her eyes, as she works out plans and options. I always find myself hoping they are in my favor.

"Next is Judith. She is extremely friendly and tirelessly giving, and does not like credit for any of the good deeds she carries out, no matter how long and trying the task may be. However, beneath her friendly exterior lies a rock-solid, unchangeable hardness. If you want her to change direction, she will smile and roll right over you.

"Then there is Sueann, like the others, giving and creative, and also a very hard worker. You won't find a lazy bone in her body; if you need anything from a flower arrangement to a ditch being dug, she's your person. You can ask her to do a job, but don't try to tell her how to do it; if it's her job, then it's HER JOB. Just leave her alone and let her get it done her way.

"There is Frances. She is a stalwart in the church. Sometimes I think she's there more than I am. She is always willing to help in any situation, but like her sisters, she can be like a dog with a bone, although she might be more like a wolf with a fresh deer kill. You always must watch your hand; if she perceives you've wronged her or anyone she cares about, you just might get mauled.

"Patricia is the lady we just met. Although all the sisters are great cooks, Patricia will always go above and beyond to make sure people are fed and fed well, but as you can see, she's a bit overcautious and untrusting, almost to the point of paranoia, especially if it involves someone she cares about.

"Margarette is next, the most gregarious of the bunch. If you have a simple little idea and ask her help or even just her opinion, it will suddenly blow up into an event whether you want it to or not, but again, don't wrong her or anyone she feels a need to protect or you're likely to get a pleasant smile as a blade slips between your ribs.

"Lastly is Michelle, the youngest. If Margarette is the concept person behind the event, Michelle is the practical, get-it-done person. But while Margarette won't let you know she's going to get you if she wants revenge, Michelle wants you to see every moment of her payback and know exactly where it came from.

"There are also four brothers. I have not met any of them, but I have heard stories. The oldest was named Brian; he was very learned and went to work for the Vatican in its great library, where he became an expert on building and restoring the great pipe organs throughout Europe. A few years ago, he undertook the refurbishment of the organ at Westminster, where he was when he passed away from an unspecified malady.

"The second oldest was Thomas; he is remembered fondly by the village here. He appeared to have been a craftsman and tinkerer. At a very early age, he would repair simple machines for anyone who needed them. He was working at a large watermill near here when there was a mysterious explosion that leveled the mill. Some say he was trying to build a machine that used steam to make a wagon move without horses. His sisters said the only thing he hated more than horses was chickens.

"The third son, Christopher, is said to have learned herblore from an old crone some claimed was a witch, yet everyone went to her if they had a family member who was sick. Christopher was well on his way to becoming a healer in his own right when, while riding to help a family with a sick child, he fell from his horse, struck his head, and died.

"The youngest son, Anthony, fell in with a poor lot and was often in trouble in his youth; he left the village as a young man. No one knows for sure what happened to him, but it is rumored he was hanged for poaching in the Kings Woods, although others say he signed on as a deckhand on some ship and left France.

"I can see I'm boring you with village gossip, yet I didn't want to talk to you about our mutual friends out in the open, but now that we have arrived at the parsonage, let us go inside and eat, and you can talk while I listen."

As Father Lull placed plates piled with food before them, Mary commenced telling the tale of her, Odo, Sir Henry, and Father Thomas after they split from the rest of the group. Father Lull broke into peals of laughter when Mary told him about meeting his acolyte Jon on the road and said, "So that is where he disappeared to. I'm sorry for him and shouldn't laugh. He really fooled me, and that doesn't happen often, or so I like to think. I had no idea he was so angry with me. I'm sorry, please continue."

Mary said, "That really is about it. A couple of days later, we arrived here and met you."

Father Lull said, "That is quite the adventure you two have undergone just to arrive two days late, but maybe I can remove some of that sting." Father Lull then told Mary what happened to Sir William, Sergeant Bertrand, and Louis. Mary was visibly shocked to hear of Sargent Bertrand's death and needed a few minutes to compose herself while Derrick placed a hand gently on her shoulder in a rather uncomfortable manner. Although she barely knew Sergeant Bertrand, she couldn't help but think of him as her rescuer.

When Father Lull got to the spot in the story about the hidden storage facility, he paused for a few moments. Then he seemed to resolve some inner conflict and said more to himself than them, "I suppose it doesn't really matter anymore." Then he abruptly stood up and said, "Follow me."

Soon all three of them were standing in the underground vault. As Derrick, Mary, and Father Lull walked along the rows of shelves stacked with bags and small wooden boxes of coins and other items, all in some disarray. Father Lull continued the story, "After Lord Groombridge and his men left Rennes-le-Chateau, I released the three Templars. They had heard nothing, being shut up down here, and were quite anxious. We wasted little time gathering the maps and the few possessions the three men had, and then left on the road to the coast near Salses, where Admiral Gregory had his ships waiting. Admiral Gregory, William, and Louis boarded one of the ships and sailed on to their next bit of business. There are three other ships there, and the good Admiral sent some of the sailors here to help me load up all this and return to the ships. I am responsible for overseeing the transfer of this wealth to a new location. Now here is where I have a question for you. Would you two be interested in accompanying me on this little undertaking? Don't answer now, let me finish telling you what I can. I cannot tell you where we are heading yet, but it will involve some days of sea travel and no little amount of hazard. You two have displayed a great deal of courage and cunning. I would appreciate the help you two could provide, and the company would also be welcome. I must say, Derrick, I have met few men who have piqued my curiosity more than you, not to mention that I have not heard you say one word so far, which indicates you are a perfect traveling companion for someone like me who can't seem to stop talking once I start. And I start often.

"Jon was supposed to have come with me, although he never knew that. Father Thomas was to take over for me here while I traveled to make arrangements before the money and other items were to be transported, but circumstances have changed those plans. I don't know how much Father Thomas knew about our little town, but from the letter Grand Master Jacques de Molay sent me, he knew little, if anything, about the facility here. It appears Sir William's concerns about the man were well-founded. So, what do you two have to say? Are you up for a little more adventure?"

Derrick, who finally found his tongue, said, "I won't need to think about it, Father. If Mary decides to go, I will go; if not, then I will not."

Father Lull looked to Mary, who was gaping at Derrick in open astonishment, then back to Derrick and said with a grin, "Oh my."

Chapter 12

Louis took to being on board the ship very easily; he loved the wind and spray on his face, as well as the feeling of rapid movement it gave him as he stood at the prow of the ship. He was intrigued by all the many and varied tasks it took to make the vessel move where and how Admiral Gregory wanted it to. It also affected him almost to his core when Admiral Gregory casually mentioned, "From the Ocean or Sea, you can travel anywhere in the world. I always feel like a freed prisoner when I start on a voyage. I do enjoy some of the pleasantries and conveniences of being landed, but within a day or two, I began to desire the feel of a rolling deck and the taste of the sea air."

William, on the other hand, did not take well to traveling at sea. He began vomiting over the side before the ship even left its moorings. Gregory told him, "It will be better once the ship starts moving. A bobbing ship is much worse on the gut than one that is cutting through the swell."

William did not agree, and as it turned out, things did not improve. Sailors aboard chuckled at his discomfort and offered a wide variety of recommendations to cure his ailment. William was told to "Look at the horizon." "Drink a bit of rum mixed with a spoonful of seawater." "Eat some greasy food." "Avoid greasy food." And one helpful individual said, "Climb the mast to its highest point and lash yourself to it until your stomach rolls with, instead of against, the motion of the ship." The sailor added, "But make sure if you have to vomit, you're not facing into the wind and that you are not above my head." None of the methods he tried worked, and he soon grew too weak and miserable to try any of the other cures. He found a dark storage room in the hold of the ship where he hid from everyone and lay down, just wishing he would die.

After four days of being at sea, they reached their destination. By then, Louis had joined in and was working as hard as any of the sailors aboard the ship. He was climbing aloft and helping to set and haul in or unfurl the sails; he had learned several knots from the deckhands and had learned the name, location, and use of the various lines and tackle.

As they approached their destination, William was just beginning to feel like a human again, but had to be very careful about what he ate, where he looked, and how quickly he turned his head. He was the third one over the side to get in the longboat for the ride ashore. As the sailors guided the boat to ride the waves to shore, William was certain they would soon capsize and all drown, while Louis loved it.

William's stomach felt almost instantly better as soon as he set foot on shore, although he did have trouble walking. His mind kept telling him that the land was rolling back and forth, and he kept feeling as though he needed to correct for a movement that no longer existed.

Admiral Gregory slapped William on the back and said, "You'll get used to it. The next time we put to sea, you won't be nearly as sick and for probably only half the time." Then he walked on past.

William stared at his back as he walked up the shore and said, "Next time?"

Waiting for the men from the boat were about a dozen others standing just above the surf line. All but one of the men wore kilts with a pattern of green and blue with orange and white lines running through it.

Admiral Gregory led William and Louis up to the men waiting for them. There were two standing in front of the group; the one in the kilt was a large, muscular man. He was at least six feet tall and had flaming red hair and a beard to match; over his shoulder, in a scabbard on his back, William could see the hilt of what appeared to be a great sword or possibly a bastard sword. The man next to him was the only man in the reception party who did not wear a kilt; he was shorter and less bulky, but by his bearing, he was clearly a soldier, and William was certain this man was a Templar. His beard was so neatly trimmed and close cut to his face; it appeared little more than a shadow, and his hair was as black as ink. Neither man looked happy to see them.

Admiral Gregory walked first to the large man in the kilt and held his hands out, palms toward the kilted man. The large man glared at him, his hands on his hips and an angry scowl on his face. Suddenly, he lunged forward, clutched Gregory by the shoulders, and hugged him as a broad grin broke on his face, and said, "I see the sea gods have seen fit to vomit you back on my shores again."

Gregory, clearly having expected the exuberant greeting, grasped the big man's forearm as the brief hug ended, then said, "Cinead! I see you've not taken up a shawl and a seat by the fire to spend your final years in peace like you said you intended to do when we last parted."

Cinead said, "Too many Englishmen to kill and not enough true Scots to do the culling."

Gregory then went to the man without the kilt and said, "Sir Jules, I would like to present Sir William de Sevrey and his squire Louis. This is Sir Jules des Morvan, Preceptor of Inverness."

William stepped forward, stood erect, and said, "Sir Jules, I don't believe we have previously met." William held his right hand out palm up, expecting Sir Jules to do the same and grasp forearms. Instead, Jules simply held his gaze neutral and didn't move or speak.

As the silence drew on for an uncomfortable moment, Jules finally said, "It is customary for a knight to offer some form of respect, at least a slight bow, when one greets another knight of a higher office."

William was completely taken by surprise. Although what Jules said was true among the courts and other knightly Orders, it was long held that titles of office within the Templars were titles of responsibility, not necessarily respect or higher rank. It was often said within the Templars that a knight was a knight and that titles didn't demand respect but conveyed a level of responsibility. Although many of the ranks carried a level of authority so that the chain of command was clearly maintained, only a very few, like Grand Master or Commander of the Vault of Acre, required any displays of respect for the individual's superior position, and even that was kept to a minimum. A Preceptor was a teacher, and while he was instructing fledgling knights and squires, he was to be obeyed and respected; it was not a higher rank and did not elevate Jules above any other knight Templar.

William decided to show the respect this knight felt he deserved as an expedient way to end the uncomfortable stalemate, so he bowed his head slightly and said, "I beg your pardon, Sir Jules. I have been sick these past few days while at sea and am not yet thinking clearly."

Sir Jules did not even nod to show any sign of respect to Sir William. Instead, he asked, "Why is it you have come so late? I was told to expect you some weeks ago. No word reached me that you would be late, so I was left to worry about the cargo you carry and that of your men."

Before William could respond, Commander Gregory said, "Well, young Jules, I am sorry that you had to lose sleep over your concern for me and these others. You may not be aware of this, but there are happenings in France that have made travel difficult for us Templars."

Jules stiffened as if slapped. For Gregory to call him 'young' and not to use the honorific 'Sir' was clearly a jab at his authority, and Sir Jules knew full well the situation in France, just as Commander Gregory knew he did. It also rankled Sir Jules that Gregory was not a true Knight but only a Sergeant-at-Arms who had risen to the office of Commander of the Vault of Acre and was considered the Admiral of the Templar Fleet, which was one of the most respected offices within the Templars. Although officially a Sergeant-at-Arms and a Knight were usually considered equals in the Templars, many Knights, such as Jules, felt that the fact that they had been born of Noble birth put them above the Sergeants who had been born commoners.

Jules, in a voice laced with burning anger, said, "I believe it would have been within your abilities to let me know of your arrival. The only advanced warning we had of your arrival came when one of our scouts noticed your ship was entering the harbor."

Commander Gregory stepped in front of Jules and leaned over him slightly and said, "I'm not certain who, if anyone, informed you that you are in command here. Let me make this clear. If I were here to learn heraldry, I would be bound to listen to you prattle on, but here and now, I see no reason to put up with your arrogant manner." Then the Commander walked further inland, not waiting for anyone else.

Jules turned instantly red-faced and was still debating how to respond when everyone else started to follow the Commander. Cinead waited a moment until Sir William had reached where he stood, then He put a big arm around William's shoulders and, with an undercurrent of laughter in his voice, said, "Ah, but you Templars are a prickly bunch. I'm Cinead of the house Sinclair, laddie. Welcome to my home. But leave our daughters and wives alone, or I'll have to disembowel you. That goes for you, too." Cinead said with a smile over his shoulder to Louis, who was just a step behind them.

Chapter 13

Thomas was standing before Brother Jaye and the other two brothers of the Inquisition. Brother Jaye was showing the only obvious displays of anger Father Thomas had seen in him over the many weeks he had spent with the Inquisitor. Every time Thomas started to explain what had happened, Brother Jaye interrupted him. Brother Jaye was shouting, "I don't think you understand the difficult situation you have placed us in due to your incompetence. That young man was one of the main pieces of evidence that we had to take before His Holiness to convince him to pass a Bull that would condemn the Templars everywhere, and you let him die."

Thomas was finally able to respond, "I am terribly sorry, I tried to stop him, but…"

Brother Jaye again interrupted with a little less volume in his still angry voice, "You tried to stop him? He was one man; how difficult could it have been?"

Father Thomas replied, "You all know how troubled he was. After seeing the head, he became even more unhinged. He ran from me, and by the time I caught up to him, he was already about to leap off the wall. I tried to talk to him, to tell him God would not forgive him if his final act was to take his own life, but as I drew almost within reach to grab him, he jumped. I deeply regret this setback, and I know it is not as effective as if spoken by Odo himself, but I can act as a firsthand witness before the Pope of all that Odo told me. There are some things he told me before he ran off that I have not had the opportunity to share with you yet."

Brother Jaye said impatiently, "Well, what is it that he told you? Get on with it."

Thomas tried to swallow, but there was no moisture in his mouth. He knew that what took place in the next few minutes would likely determine his future. He tried to clear his dry throat and said, "Brother Jaye, if I may request an indulgence. What I have to say is of a delicate nature, and I believe if you and I could speak in private, it might be for the best."

Brother Jaye looked as though he might explode in a fit of anger again. Father Thomas could visibly see as the storm rose and then subsided across the brother's face in the span of two or three seconds. Brother Jaye took a breath and said in a voice struggling to remain calm, "As you wish." Then he nodded toward the door to the other two members of the inquisition.

As the two left the room, Thomas asked Brother Jaye, "Might I have some water? My throat is very dry."

Brother Jaye filled a cup with some water from a pitcher on the table and said, "Your usefulness to us has taken a severe turn for the worse, Father Thomas. I hope for your sake you have something very useful to tell me."

Thomas took a long drink of water and said, "Again, I apologize for my lack of vigilance with Odo; I had no idea he would do such a thing. While we were talking earlier in the evening, before he ran from me, he told me a few things of great consequence. He said he had been afraid to tell us earlier because he thought he would be punished, but after seeing the head, he knew he had to do all he could to stop the Templars. He told me that he had on one occasion been asked to bring wine to a chamber in the bowels of the commandery where the Knights and Sergeants-at-Arms were holding a private meeting. The Grand Master, Jacques de Molay, was in attendance. He said that normally he would not be allowed in the room, yet this time he was told to enter. When he entered the room, he found it illuminated by flickering candlelight. To his shock and horror, he slowly became aware that several of those present were in various stages of undress. When one of the Knights noticed him carrying the wine, he took the bottles and directed him to the Grand Master, who was seated on a throne-like chair. He said the Grand Master greeted him in a very informal and friendly manner. When the Grand Master noticed the shock on Odo's face, he told Odo, "I'm sure this seems very strange to you, my son, but this is just part of the initiation rites to the secrets of our Order. These are the methods we use to help instill a sense of genuine brotherhood. Let me demonstrate. Remove your shirt."

Odo, not believing it would be right to refuse the Grand Master of their Order, did as was requested. When he stood shirtless, the Grand Master kissed him on the small of his back and on the navel. Then he said, "Now you do likewise with me."

As the Grand Master started to remove his shirt, Odo fled just as Joseph fled Potiphar's wife. He said one of the Knights stepped in front of Odo to stop him, but the Grand Master said, "Let him go. We will make a true Templar of him when the time is right; he is too young to understand yet."

On another occasion, he and another squire named Louis were removing the Crucifix from the front of the church so that it could be repainted. A Sergeant Bertrand was overseeing them, and according to Odo, the Sergeant was reclining on the altar and drinking wine. As they lowered the cross, a rope parted, and the cross fell the last few feet and broke. He said that he was terrified by what had happened, but that Sergeant Bertrand only laughed and said, "Don't worry about that, Odo, we do much worse to the Cross in the dark. You will see once you are initiated into the true Templars."

There are more stories of this kind that he told me, but these are good examples. Odo spoke of these and many other stories in the hours we spoke before he took his life. I believe it was the fear of Baphomet, in part, that drove him to finally reveal to me the things he had previously been unwilling to share. I believe it was the feeling of shame from these instances that led him to commit such an unforgivable act as killing himself. The many stories he shared with me in private must have worn on his soul and pushed him over the edge. Stories that I'm sure you will find quite beneficial in your case against the Templars when we speak to the Pope.

Brother Jaye did not fail to notice the use of "we" when Father Thomas referred to visiting the Pope. He was not at all happy that the crazy young man, Odo, had died, but Thomas was correct; there was always the concern that Odo would change his story or blurt something out at the wrong moment that could hurt their case against the Templars. Odo was just too difficult to control. With Father Thomas, he could be more confident that he would say what he was told to say. The only concern he had with Father Thomas was that he was absolutely certain that if the good Father saw an opportunity to betray him, he would obviously take it. He would have to ensure that Father Thomas understood how things worked and that Thomas believed his best path was to remain loyal to Brother Jaye.

Brother Jaye smiled his shark-like smile at Father Thomas and said, "This may suit our needs. Odo was our best source, but he was always a bit unpredictable. Perhaps a more controlled and thoughtful mouthpiece, such as yourself, would be for the best. I apologize for my earlier outbursts. I believe the two of us will make a good team and work together to remove this scourge from the midst of Christendom."

Father Thomas allowed a brief smile to cross his face as he said, "I am here only to serve Mother Church as God sees fit to use this humble vessel."

Chapter 14

Henry was carrying a bucket of water from the well to the kitchen for the cooks. Two Hospitaller knights entered the front gate, accompanied by a third man dressed in rags. The raggedy man had a long, scruffy beard and was filthy; he seemed to be all skin and bones, yet he was still able to walk under his own power, albeit with a shuffle of his feet to keep moving. As the man drew closer to Henry, he realized he knew this man; he was Garrard de La Languedoc! Sir Garrard had been locked up with Henry and had shown great strength and courage by holding true to The Templars, even under appalling torture. Later, he and Henry were isolated in a cell together for some time, until a cardinal had separated them. Henry resisted the urge to go to Sir Garrard and help him, even though he was curious to find out what had happened to him after they had been separated while in captivity.

It was nearly a week before Henry saw Garrard again. Garrard was helping the cooks prepare a meal. He had been cleaned up and was now clean-shaven, and although he appeared steadier on his feet, he was still quite thin. It was almost another week before Henry had an opportunity to speak to Garrard.

They were both in the stables, mucking out the stalls. Henry said, "Sir Garrard, it's me, Henry."

Garrard did not look up from what he was doing but responded in a low voice, "Yes, I know you, Henry. I noticed you the day I arrived. And Henry, I would remind you, I, like you, am no longer a member of the chivalry, so I am just Garrard. I have no right to the title of 'Sir.'"

Henry said, "I am glad to see you are still alive. Have you been held as a prisoner by the King and the Inquisition this whole time?"

Garrard, while continuing to rake horse manure out of a stall, said, "Most of the time, yes. After we were separated, I was taken back to a cell alone and received slightly better care. Then a group of inquisitors sent by the Pope arrived, and they returned me to the rest of the Templar population. At first, they merely questioned us, and I thought maybe these inquisitors wouldn't be as bad as those who questioned you and me. After receiving no confessions, they decided to start torturing us. They brought in a rack, the sight of which made several men confess instantly. The first man, I do not recall the poor fellow's name, refused to confess as the windless was turned slowly, and he was stretched. We could hear the popping of his joints over his screams as his wrists and ankles were dislocated. Eventually, I was selected, but instead of the rack, they used the strappado. My arms were bound behind me, then a long rope was attached around my wrists; the other end was passed up through a beam in the ceiling. I was hauled off the ground by my bound wrists, arms behind my back, and lifted some 10 feet in the air, and then they released the rope. I dropped until just a few inches from the ground, where I was stopped abruptly. My arms felt like they would detach from my shoulders, and the pain was shocking and severe. As I still would confess to nothing, they attached some weights to my testicles and repeated the drop twice more. I still would not confess. There were two more days of torture, but I was no longer questioned. Most confessed to at least something. Spitting on the cross was most common, although they all claimed that they only spat beside it and not on it. The other was indecent kissing of the navel and spine. Some were so afraid they confessed to worship of idols and other worse sacrilege. I believe they felt that if they confessed to greater crimes, they would receive better treatment.

"In the end, six others and I, who had maintained our innocence, were selected to be taken before the Pope. We were brought before the Holy Father and several Cardinals. We were all questioned, and we all explained that we knew nothing of any of the crimes being leveled against our Order. We were asked how we could reconcile our denial of the charges brought against the Templars when most of the Order had already confessed, including the Grand Master himself. We began to mention the torture we underwent, but were interrupted and told that there was no excuse by one of the Cardinals, that the tortures that were used followed the guidelines of the Holy Roman Church and were directed by men of God to encourage the truth, not to cause any lasting injuries. These methods were only used to aid honest men to cleanse their souls.

"One of my fellow Templars, who could barely walk and could not raise either arm above his head because of the 'encouragement' he endured, explained how the only men to question him were men of the King and that the priest who was present only took notes. In addition, all the men who questioned him were very drunk and seemed to delight in the pain they inflicted. Some of the Cardinals appeared not to believe what we said, but most of them seemed to be upset when we described our treatment. The Pope, who never spoke during the proceedings, seemed to look upon us as if He were sympathetic to our pain. We were kept in Avignon for a week and then returned to Paris, where, once again, I was held as a prisoner by the king's men. After another month of imprisonment, I was given the option to enter the Knight Hospitallers as a novice monk, and here I am.

Henry said, "I do not understand how the Church can stand by and allow this to continue. It angers me that good men, such as yourself, are suffering for no reason. I am glad you are here and in reasonably good health. Do you still maintain the innocence of our Order?"

Garrard paused for a moment, then replied, "I do not know of any accusation against our Order. The Knights Hospitaller are in good standing with the Holy See and the King of France as far as I am aware."

Henry stopped what he was doing and looked at Garrard, who was still raking manure and looking only at the ground. He felt he knew this man and believed he was still a Templar at heart, but the mistreatment he had endured could have changed him. After looking around to make sure they were still alone, he decided to push a little further and said, "Some of the former Templars that are here have accepted the conversion from a Templar to the Hospitallers as a way of getting away from the kings men and want nothing more than to be left alone, to be a slave to the new Order they have been adopted into. Others still feel as though they are

Templars. They accepted the offer to become an apprentice Hospitaller as a means to escape captivity where their voice was effectively silenced in the hopes that they might find a way to clear the name of the Templars."

There was a long silence as the two men worked, then Garrard finally said, "I wish both groups of men well in their endeavors. I believe I am done here. I will go to discover what further task the Sergeant has for me to do." With that, Garrard left Henry to finish scooping horse shit into the wheelbarrow.

Chapter 15

It took just over a week to transport all the money and possessions in the hidden alcove under the church in Rennes-le-Chateau to the waiting ships offshore near Salses. Mary, Derrick, and Father Lull worked from dawn until sundown, helping the sailors and many of the townspeople who came out to help. The loading of the ships was left in charge of Captain Timm, who was in command of the remaining three ships after Admiral Gregory departed with William and Louis.

Finally, as Father Lull, Mary, Derrick, and Captain Timm watched from shore as the final load was being taken out to the ships, Father Lull looked at Mary and Derrick and said, "So what do you think? Are you two going to join me on this adventure?"

Mary shook her head, placed her hands on her hips, and said in an admonishing tone, "Father Lull, I believe we have answered you on several occasions already. I am beginning to wonder if you would rather we did not accompany you. Just to be abundantly clear, we are coming with you. If the ship sinks and you are clinging to some flotsam, and we are on another, we will join you on your piece of debris. We are going with you, Father Lull. Stop asking."

Father Lull laughed and said, "Okay. I just worry that you will change your mind. I have grown fond of the two of you and would hate to have to undertake this job without you two to assist me."

Derrick asked Captain Timm in his usual quiet monotone, "We loaded a lot of weight onto those three ships. Are you sure they won't sink?"

The captain didn't answer right away. He normally replied to questions like this from landlubbers who questioned his ships with a lot of bluster and blow so they wouldn't bother him any further, but over the last few days, he had been impressed by the scarred young man. When Captain Timm first met Derrick, he thought he was either a bit dim or possibly just a coward since he seemed to let Mary speak for him most of the time. He soon learned that he didn't speak unless absolutely necessary, and he rarely needed to. He was also a hard worker, and as the work continued, they all discovered how resourceful he was. At one location on the path from Rennes-le-Chateau to the waiting ships, there was a steep fifty-foot drop that had to be negotiated by a dangerous switchback trail. After the second day of slowly carrying the heavy loads down the dangerous switchbacks, Derrick spent his evening fashioning a pair of crude but functional blocks and tackle. Then, before anyone else was awake, he carried them out to the switchbacks, where he fashioned a lift to a newly fallen tree he positioned across a narrow canyon a short distance from the top of the switchbacks.

The next morning, when they arrived at the site, Derrick was just finishing his work and showed them how to load the heavy supplies onto the platform he had fashioned from large branches and lower them to the bottom. This saved them a great deal of time and significantly reduced the risk of serious injury. When Timm asked him where he learned how to make the blocks. Derrick quietly said he'd only seen them in use the day before on the ships, as they were used for hauling the items being brought to the ship. He said he'd made and used simple pulleys before, but had never seen them used in combination like that. Since they didn't look too difficult to make, he thought he'd give it a try.

Captain Timm finally answered Derrick, "No, lad, the ships won't sink. In fact, all that weight will help the ships move through the water more efficiently. The smallest of my three ships could carry three times that weight without making her ride low enough to create any concern about her seaworthiness. My ship alone has carried more than one hundred and fifty tons of cargo."

Mary piped in then, "Captain, why do you always call your ships 'her' and 'she'? Is it because you force the ship to do what you want, like men seem to think they can do to women?"

Timm replied, "No, my lady, it's because we love them. The Sea is also a woman that we sailors love and can't live without. It's hard for a landlubber to understand, but I can hardly bear being out of sight of a body of water. The sea and the ships we ride upon when we travel give us sailors freedom that can't be found on land. A cabin boy at sea has more freedom than an Earl on his own land.

We do not force a ship to our will; we work with her to guide her to our destination, just as any true man would do with his lady."

Mary said almost under her breath, "Haven't met too many 'true men', I guess." Then in a clear voice, she added before anyone could comment, "When do we set sail? And are you ready to tell us where we are going yet?"

Father Lull said, "When we set sail, it is up to the captain, and as for our destination, we are going to make our first stop in Germany and then work our way to Norway. From there, I am not certain it depends on several other factors, many of which I don't believe have been decided upon yet."

Captain Timm said, "I would like to sail at first light tomorrow morning. We are ready to sail, but I'd like to top off our freshwater and food supplies. We must travel quite a way south, then south-west before we can turn north, and with the way things are, I'd rather not have to send anyone ashore until we are well north of France."

"Well, we can go for a walk at least before we go aboard. The sun is about to set, and I, for one, would like to watch it with my feet on the ground before we go take to the ship," Father Lull said as he took Mary's arm and started off down the beach, with Derrick following.

Chapter 16

Louis found he enjoyed being among the Scottish a great deal. The men were all full of life; they enjoyed laughing and joking and delighted in games of strength and guile. And although there was always an undercurrent of a threat of violence in many interactions, Louis quickly grew used to it. Mostly, what Louis liked about the Scotts was that they didn't mind his talking. They made fun of the fact that he could carry on a one-sided conversation "longer than an old woman," but they still listened and usually offered their opinion, which often consisted of recommendation like; "You need a woman, but stay away from my daughters, or I'll open you from groin to gullet." or "Just kill um' and be done with it" or "That's nothing laddie, let me tell you about the time I…." At first, Louis didn't like all the overt threats to life and limb. He soon realized it was partly just the way they spoke, so that others would understand not to try and take advantage of them, but also that it had something to do with their lives as Scotsmen. They were all deeply connected to "their country" and were violently angry and somewhat embarrassed that England had stolen it from them.

One of the phrases Louis learned to love, and that he remembered fondly the rest of his life, was, "You're a long time dead." It puzzled him the first dozen or so times he heard it, but he finally put it together. They were saying that death is forever, and that life is short, don't waste it, have fun while you can. This was the long-term lesson he took from his time among the Scots.

Although they had leaders, their ideas about obedience to the leaders seemed somewhat open to interpretation. When it came to religion, there was also freedom from authority. They all claimed to be Christian, but their form of Christianity seemed a mix of Catholicism and folk magic. This initially really bothered Louis, but he soon found that he truly enjoyed hearing stories about the Green Man, Finn and his soldiers, the Fianna, and the Kelpies, who seemed to be some kind of spirit horse that enjoyed drowning people. The most intriguing mix of magic and Christianity for Louis occurred one evening when he noticed a group of villagers gathered near the water's edge. They had just made a batch of ale, so he went to join them, but as he grew closer, he noticed the gathering was unusually somber and quiet, so he kept quiet and watched. They didn't seem to mind his presence even though he was the only Templar among them, but none spoke to him. Then one of the women took a large cup of ale and offered it, rather reverently, to Finlay, one of the largest men Louis had ever met, but rather than call him by his real name, they called him the "Seonaidh." Finlay, or the Seonaidh, then waded out into the water and ceremonially poured the ale in the frigid sea. Following the pouring of the ale into the water, they went to the local church, lit a candle, and stood silently for some time. Then, they put the candle out and went to a local field, laughing and joking in the manner Louis was more accustomed to seeing these people. They had moved the batch of ale, and they all drank eagerly. When Louis asked them about this ceremony, he was told that it was a prayer of sorts to bring a bountiful harvest. When asked to whom they prayed and who or what the Seonaidh was? He was told to "Shut ye geggie and drink more ale." Louis found it hard to believe the local priest allowed these practices.

Louis had lots of questions, but no one seemed willing to answer them to his satisfaction. Soon, he grew strangely comfortable with the mix of the Church and beliefs in the power of nature. There was more freedom in the worship, more joy, and in some ways, he felt there was more honesty. Yet after a time, he did miss the majesty and the feeling of holiness that sometimes overcame him during a high Mass in a Cathedral.

Louis knew some of the men who were lay-brothers were considering remaining in Scotland when the rest of the Templars moved on. As lay-brothers, they had taken no permanent vows to the Templars. Louis realized that since he had not yet taken vows, he was among those who could remain here among these people whom he felt very at home with and free himself from his link with the Templars. As a youth, he had aspired to become a Knight Templar, wielding the twin-edged sword of justice and faith against the Church's enemies. Now there was little chance of another crusade in the Holy Lands. And apparently, the Church seemed on the verge of dismantling the Templar Order. He didn't know what to do. He could go to William and talk to him about his concerns, but although he knew William would accept his choice to stay, he would never understand it. William was a Templar to the core. Oddly enough, Louis wished Sergeant Bertrand were here to talk with. The old, grizzled warrior was rough and intimidating, but he seemed a bit more open-minded about things outside the Templar Order.

Chapter 17

Henry and the other former Templars gathered by candlelight in the dark underground room for the fifth time. Only one new member had been added to their small group, but Henry was still hopeful Garrard would come around and join their numbers.

Father Anthony said, "I know we have discussed the need for secrecy for our group, but if we expect to gather more compatriots to our cause, we must come up with a way of reaching out to other former Templars that will not put the group at risk."

Henry replied, "I agree, Father, but I don't know how to do that. We are given little time to speak with one another, and even then, there is always the fear that we will be overheard. The only place we can speak openly and at length is here."

Father Anthony said, "Yes, I realize that. I have been thinking about this for some time, and I believe I have the beginnings of a solution. I thought if we could come up with a word or gesture that, if viewed by anyone who was not a Templar, would appear to be of no consequence, but for those of us who are Templars, it would carry meaning. For instance, I thought we could use the word 'Boaz' as we encounter another former brother. Anyone overhearing that would not understand, and if we are questioned, we could just say we were greeting one another, saying 'bonjour.'" But we Templars know the meaning behind the word, referring to one of the pillars of the porch of Solomon's Temple, the pillar of strength, since we all know it to be one of the words of unity used within our Order. If the former Templar responds by repeating the word back, he may be inclined toward our cause; if not, we can rule him out."

Jamison, the Master Mason, said, "We masons use many hand signs while building, especially when moving large stones. Often, those directing the placement of the stones must be some distance away to have enough perspective to line things up properly. Due to distance and the surrounding noise, we have developed several hand signals. For instance, if we notice a problem and want the workers to stop, we place our fingers together, raise them above our heads, and make a large "O" with our arms; the workers then know they need to stop. Perhaps we can use something like that, only less obvious."

Henry, after a moment's thought, said, "What if we inconspicuously made an 'O' simply with our hands? We could use it to silently alert another of our newly established secret Order of the Templars that they need to be cautious. Father, I believe this idea of yours holds great potential. Perhaps we could develop an entire secret language of unobtrusive keywords, hand gestures, and handshakes."

Victor de Lorraine asked, "I know I'm changing the subject, but does anyone have any news regarding the King's charges against our Order? Or even why he is doing this?"

Peter de Rhone replied, "It's obvious why he is doing it. King Philip IV wants our money; he's broke, and he wants to maintain his lavish lifestyle."

Father Anthony said, "I'm afraid there is more to it than that. Some of you may know that a few years ago, the King requested to be made an official member of the Knights Templar. This horrified everyone in leadership because we knew the King coveted not only the Templar wealth and holdings, but he wished to command our armies. This attempt to join us was a thinly veiled ploy to soon force his way into becoming our Grand Master and make the Templars his servants. It's no secret that King Philip considers himself semi-divine and believes he has greater authority than the Pope. The leadership of the Templars denied His request on the grounds that, as the King of France, it would not be possible for Him to obey the Rule. This rejection did not make the King happy, and I believe this, in part, has led him to take action against us.

"Additionally, Sir Peter is correct that the King needs money. He has already used several strong-arm tactics to gain funds. Last year, he arrested Jews and seized their assets and then kicked them out of the country so they couldn't try to get their properties back. More recently, he debased the coinage and decided to tax the clergy at half their annual income, even though it was clearly not within his power to do so. He believes that, due to his being the 'Divine King of France,' He can do anything he pleases."

"Including arresting and imprisoning a Monastic Order answerable only to the Pope," added Sir Henry.

Chapter 18

Brother Jaye and Father Thomas traveled to see the Pope at the orders of King Philip IV of France. They brought with them volumes of confessions from numerous Knights, Sergeants, and other members of standing within the Templars. They also carried the skull, which Brother Jaye had ordered to be placed in a small chest he had specially built to contain the item. Brother Jaye had decided it would be better to present the object of Templar worship as something the Order had considered of great value, not an item tossed aside in an underground storeroom. The chest he ordered built for it resembled a treasure chest. He had the craftsman line the inside with velvet and even had an ornate lock fashioned into the chest, and Father Jaye was given the only key. Father Jaye had personally informed the craftsman who built it to do all the work himself and tell no one else about it. He wanted the Templar cross carved into the lid, and then he had the craftsman "age" the chest so that it looked as if the Templars had carried it and the revered object inside from the Holy Land. Brother Jaye did not want to leave the skull with the craftsman, but the man had convinced Brother Jaye that if he wanted the chest to appear made for this particular skull, he would need it to fashion the base and lid so that the velvet lining fit it perfectly.

Brother Jaye and Father Thomas spent all their time preparing for their audience with the Holy Father. The King expected this meeting to be the capstone that would finally get Pope Clement V to call for the arrest of all the Templars within the Holy Roman Empire. Both Brother Jaye and Thomas felt the great weight of responsibility that pressed down on their shoulders because of the King's expectations.

The night before the two were to depart for Avignon, Brother Jaye sent soldiers under his command to the craftsman who built the chest to collect it. The craftsman had just completed the chest that day. Immediately after taking possession of the chest and skull, the soldiers placed the craftsman under arrest and delivered him to the dungeons that the Inquisition used.

Immediately after arriving in Avignon, Brother Jaye and Father Thomas were instructed to wait in the antechamber, as the Pope wished to see them immediately. Apparently, "immediately" meant as soon as they could be fit into the Pope's very busy schedule. After several hours, it began to grow dark. Father Thomas and Brother Jaye both became restless and very hungry. While Thomas amused himself by playing with a cat that had wandered in, Brother Jaye attempted to get some food for them and tried to find out when they might see the Vicar of Christ. A Fellow Priest who was also waiting watched Father Thomas playing with the cat for a few minutes and then said, "I wouldn't let the Cardinals or Pope Clement see you doing that."

Father Thomas looked up at the man and said, "What? Playing with the cat?"

The Priest replied, "Yes. The Holy Father hates cats and is rumored to believe they are a source of evil in the world."

Father Thomas thanked the Priest while he tried to shoo the cat away, as it wound its way around his legs. The cat seemed to think it was a game and refused to leave until the large doors at the end of the room opened, and Brother Jaye and Father Thomas were called forward.

They entered the room to find Pope Clement V seated on a Throne on a raised platform. There were perhaps ten Cardinals seated on ornate wooden chairs with arms and a thick cushion to sit on. The Chairs were placed officiously to either side of the Pope's platform. In front of the Pope on the floor level, two priests were seated at a table with stacks of paper, a pen, and ink. The room seemed to be all red and gold. Long red draperies covered the walls; the stone floor was covered in a massive red rug with gold designs woven into it. There were large, ornate golden candelabras scattered around the windowless room, providing most of the light. The room had one large fireplace along one wall and multiple golden braziers scattered throughout the room to provide additional light and warmth.

Brother Jaye and Father Thomas both knelt before the Pope and kissed the ring that was proffered to them.

Pope Clement V started by saying, "I would like to know why the King of France has seen fit to retain possession of MY Knights Templar and the money and other assets given to their charge as servants of the Church?"

Brother Jaye, expecting this question, said, "Your Holiness, your servant King Philip IV of France has been holding these dangerous and deceitful men and their possessions in safekeeping for You until this matter can be resolved. The King asked me to come to you with these confessions and other evidence of the vile acts and heretical practices of the Knights Templar. In the prayerful hope that You will see that it is in the best interest of Christianity that the other Kings under Your Holy Regine should also arrest and seize the Templar assets before they can escape to spread their nefarious teachings."

Pope Clement V sat in silence for a moment and then said, "I have met some of the men you have questioned; they say your methods used to extract the confessions are a bit overzealous, and that is the only reason that some of the Templars have confessed. Even under these methods, I believe there are many who have not confessed to any of the accusations and maintain the holiness and innocence of the Order."

Brother Jaye replied, "I believe, Your Holiness, that there are very few who have not confessed, and perhaps they know nothing of the secret meetings and unholy rites most of the Order have engaged in. Also, I believe you have spoken with Bernard Pelet and Esquin of Floran regarding the accusations. These two men are above reproach and have firsthand knowledge of the Templars' crimes. I also have brought with me truly damning evidence, much of it gleaned from a Templar squire who, in his innocence, witnessed much of the depravity of the Templars and their worship of evil spirits. We were even able to locate an evil idol that the Templars venerated above God Himself."

Pope Clement said, "Where is this squire?"

Brother Jaye shook his head slowly with a pained expression on his face, and said, "I am sorry, Your Holiness, but the young man was so grieved by what he witnessed and his fear of reprisals by both the Templars and spiritual forces of evil that he believed the Templars worshipped, that he took his own life." Brother Jaye made the sign of the cross and continued, "I have here with me, Father Thomas, who was himself a Templar Priest who aided King Philip in his case against the Templars. Father Thomas was also the confessor of the squire Odo before he killed himself."

The Pope looked from Brother Jaye to Father Thomas, who stood slightly behind and to the left of Brother Jaye.

Before the Pope could ask Father Thomas anything, Brother Jaye continued, "Through the squire Odo, we learned that the Templars worship a spirit called Baphomet, and we brought with us an idol that they worshiped in the spirit's image. It is a human skull that has a beard, and as you will see, it glows with an unholy light."

Brother Jaye motioned for the novices, who carried the documents and the chest containing the skull, to bring them forward. Brother Jaye then removed the key to open the chest, hoping it would work. He had not thought until this moment that perhaps he should have tested the lock before now; he had been so rushed; he had not bothered to open the chest since it was brought from the craftsman's shop. As he turned the key in the lock, he heard the satisfying 'clunk' of the latch opening. He turned the chest so that it faced the Pope and slowly raised the lid. Brother Jaye heard many of the Cardinals inhale and saw several of them make the sign of the cross out of the corner of his eye. Brother Jaye was hopeful that this skull might be enough evidence for the Pope to condemn the Templars without the need for Thomas.

After a brief silence, Pope Clement said, "I don't see any glow or a beard."

Brother Jaye shifted his position so he could see the skull. And what he saw made him boil in anger. It took him some time to recover his senses and recall where he was. He was so furious, and his mind was racing, trying to track down who was at fault and how he would punish them. The skull in the chest was no longer covered with the growth that appeared to be a beard; it seemed that someone had gone to great lengths to clean the skull, so that it almost appeared to shine as if polished. Brother Jaye was certain that the fool of a craftsman who made the chest must have thought he was doing his job by cleaning the skull, but in so doing, he cleaned off the substance that appeared to be a beard. Brother Jaye only hoped that it still glowed in the dark. He forced his anger aside and said in what he trusted was an awed tone, "I am sorry, Your Holiness, but somehow the beard that was on this skull has vanished, perhaps by supernatural means. I am sorry, but let me see if it still glows. The glow was only noticeable in the dark." Brother Jaye snapped a finger at one of the novices who retrieved a bolt of dark velvet about the size of a sleeping blanket. Brother Jaye covered the chest and himself with a thick velvet and waited. Nothing happened; Brother Jaye wanted to scream. How could he have let this happen?! Someone would pay for making him look like a fool; if the craftsman could not be adequately disciplined, then his family would pay!

Brother Jaye came out from beneath the blanket and said, "I must apologize, Your Holiness, but…I have no words. I do not understand what could have happened, but I will find out."

Then Father Thomas spoke for the first time, and to Brother Jaye, it was as if someone poured cold water over his heart. "If I may interject," Father Thomas started softly, "I may have an explanation."

Chapter 19

It was a beautiful evening at sea, and Captain Timm was at the helm by himself when Mary noticed him and walked up beside him, and they shared a quiet moment between them. Captain Timm broke the silence and commented, "It's times like these that I don't know how men can live on land."

Mary replied, "It is very relaxing, and yet, still invigorating."

Captain Timm said, "It's more than that, it's perfect. It causes a man to feel content and alive."

Mary asked Captain Timm, "What kind of boats are these?"

Captain Timm replied, "Well, to start with, they are not boats; they are ships. A boat is something you float down a river in or paddle across a pond. And secondly, are you sure you want to ask a born-and-bred seaman about his ship? We can go on in excruciating detail."

Mary laughed and said, "Yes, I am truly interested, but if you go into too much detail or I get bored, I will let you know."

Captain Timm said, "Ok, you asked for it. This ship is a Cog. Most Cogs, like this one, are single-masted and square-rigged. Cogs are typically constructed with a clinker-built hull, where the slats for the sides of the vessel overlap, starting at the bottom and working their way up. We have a stern-mounted rudder, which is a great improvement over the side rudder I first learned on. The bottom is flat, making it easy to unload when we have a nice sandy harbor where we can let the ship rest on its flat bottom. The Cogs have high sides, which help keep out water and make it difficult for anyone to try to forcibly board us. Cogs also have both stem and stern posts, which add to their strength. This particular Cog has a castle mounted both fore and stern for use in sea battles.

"The other two vessels in our flotilla are Hulks. They are similar to the Cog, but there are a few significant differences. They are reverse clinker-built, which means that during construction, the slats are installed starting at the sheer strake and overlap, working their way down toward the keel. This makes them more difficult to caulk, and it just doesn't look right to me. There are no stem or stern posts, so, to my way of thinking, they are structurally weaker than a Cog. The sides are lower, and both bow and stern rise more steeply, which I find ungainly. You will notice they have two castles fore and aft and are single-masted with a stern-mounted rudder, like us. The only advantage of a Hulk over a Cog is that the Hulk can be rowed as well as sailed, so in a sea battle or in a harbor, it is more maneuverable. But I still don't like them as much as a Cog, especially Jocelyn here."

Mary asked, "Jocelyn?"

Captain Timm replied, "This is between you, the wind, and me. Sometimes, especially late at night when it's quiet, and I'm at the helm, and no one is around, I talk to her. It's hard to believe she's not alive in those moments, and so over the years I've given her a name, Jocelyn."

Mary, with a bit of a gleam in her eyes, said, "Was there a real Jocelyn?"

Captain Timm grinned and said, "You don't think my ship is real?" When Mary refused to respond, the captain's grin broadened, and he said, "Yes, there was a real Jocelyn. Before I became a real sailor and was hired by the Templars, I ran a fishing vessel out of Calais. It was my first real command and may have been the happiest time of my life. Simple, hard, honest work. I'd spend almost all my time at sea, even though I never went far. One early afternoon after the morning fishing was done, I was in town gathering supplies while the other two men of my crew cleaned fish and repaired the nets. I noticed a young lady with a basket who seemed to be wandering around in a somewhat random manner. I was sitting out front of the bar drinking an ale. I saw her walk down the same street three times, looking around as if she were lost. Calais is not that large, and I found it hard to believe anyone could be lost. I finally approached the young lady and asked if she needed help. At first, I thought she might strike me. She was so frustrated that when I spoke to her, an angry look flashed across her face. Almost immediately, the angry expression vanished, and she visibly drooped and almost cried as she told me how she lived on a farm outside of the city and had been sent to the city by her mother to deliver some eggs to a bakery that was supposed to be around here, but she got turned around and couldn't find it. I offered to help and asked if she knew the name of the bakery. When she told me, I couldn't help but let out a bark of laughter. The bakery was right behind her with a sign hanging out on the front, plain as day. She turned to see what I was looking at and then she also laughed. As she started to turn to walk across the street to the bakery, I took her arm and said, 'Let me guide you. I wouldn't want you to get lost again.' She laughed again. Afterward, I had a drink with her, and we ate some cheese and fruit the bar sold and talked until it started to get dark, then I walked her home."

Captain Timm just stopped there, so Mary asked, "And then...?"

The captain said, "Nothing, I never saw her again. I think of her often, even to this day. The sea is my life and my love, and she allows no mistress. I cannot live on a farm, and I couldn't have her live aboard ship with me. I don't know if you've noticed, but women are not very welcome aboard a ship. The sailors will tolerate a female passenger, such as yourself, for a brief time, but long term, women are bad luck at sea."

Mary, with a bit of an edge to her voice, said, "Yes, I've noticed, in particular, that first mate, Raphael, is very clear he does not want me aboard."

Captain Timm said, "I'll have a word with him."

Mary cut him off and said, "No, you will not! I will deal with him myself, but back to Jocelyn, couldn't you have lived ashore and still fished during the day?"

Captain Timm, "Oh, many men try that, but it rarely works. Besides, even at that time, I was often at sea for several days, and I was already thinking about what lies beyond the horizon. Although I can't properly explain it to someone who hasn't heard the 'Siren Song' of the Sea, the wind and spray and the waves and the smell and taste of the sea become an irresistible call that overpowers even that of the love of a good woman. I've often thought about what might have been if I'd have pursued the flesh and blood Jocelyn, but

I'm married to this wood and sail Jocelyn, and I'm bound to her as much as she is to me."

Mary shook her head and said, "That's mosquito-buggery! That's just the type of reasoning men like to use to cover their stupidity and make it sound noble. You should have gone after the real Jocelyn." Abruptly, Mary walked away, shaking her head.

Captain Timm laughed and said quietly as his hand patted the wood of the helm, "Don't be offended, my love, she doesn't understand; perhaps one day she will. Some days, I do wonder after that other Jocelyn." Just then, the wind shifted just enough for the sail to slacken a bit and then pop with a loud 'crack' as the canvas refilled with the wind. Captain Timm smiled and said softly, "Sorry, no one can ever take me from my true Jocelyn, it was just a brief thought."

Chapter 20

Sir William ate his first good meal the evening they arrived in Scotland as the guest of Cinead Sinclair. William felt much better after eating some food. He was still a little unbalanced on his feet after the sea voyage, but he was happy to just be on land again. After the meal, William, Admiral Gregory, and Cinead went for a walk and talked about where things stood in Scotland.

They walked through the darkness as though they were three old friends out for a stroll; everyone they passed knew Cinead and greeted him, and to William's surprise, some also knew Admiral Gregory. They made their way to a low stone wall on the outskirts of the town, away from the firelights of the town and any other people.

Cinead said, "The fight for our independence began some years ago, but was not organized. Half of the Scottish nobles fought for King Edward I, while the other half fought against him. For a while, many of us rallied around William Wallace, but in 1298, after the defeat at Falkirk, Wallace resigned as Guardian of Scotland. Then, not much of significance took place in terms of actual fighting. However, a couple of years ago, the English captured Wallace with the help of some traitorous Scots. The English bastards convicted him of treason, but Wallace said during the trial, 'I could not be a traitor to Edward, for I was never his subject.' Wallace was always one to speak his mind. So, the English stripped him naked and dragged him behind horses through the streets to the Elms at Smithfield. There, they hanged him until he was almost dead, then let him get his breath and recover his senses. Once he was aware of what they were doing, the bloody bastards cut off his manhood, then slit open his belly and took out his intestines and burned them before him. After this, they beheaded him and then quartered his body. Then the damned fools in England thought it a good idea to send two of the four parts of his body to Stirling and Perth, and that finally ignited a flame in the dry tinder that is Scotland.

"Robert the Bruce and John Comyn finally decided to resolve who should be king of Scotland. At the meeting, John Comyn was killed; I won't even hazard a guess at what really took place; there are more rumors about who did what and about secret plans and lies than there are about you Templars. This I do know; I would have followed whichever loyal Scotsman stood up to kick the English out of our country. I believe either would have served, but as it turns out, Bruce came out on top. But John Comyn was killed at the hands of Robert the Bruce or his men in a Church, and that created a problem. Although Bishop Wishart absolved him of any wrongdoing, Pope Clement V excommunicated him, but not before Robert was crowned King Robert I of Scotland.

"It didn't go well at first. Bruce's army was defeated at Methven. Shortly after that, his wife, daughter, sisters, and one brother, Neil, were captured by Edward I. They hung, drew, and quartered Neil just like Wallace. There were a few skirmishes here and there where we, the Scots, mostly prevailed, but then came the fight at Loudoun Hill, where we kicked the English army's ass. Then, glory to God and the Green Man, Longshanks, Edward I died, leaving the campaign to his son, Edward II.

"There was a pause in our fight with England while Edward II took control, so we started North with about three thousand men to either fight or persuade the Comyn's to join us against our common foe. We're at a standstill now. King Robert the Bruce has been ill for a while. Men are starting to disappear, heading home for the winter, I suppose; they are probably all telling themselves they will return before the 1308 campaign starts. We'll be lucky to have one thousand men come Spring. That is, unless you Templars hang around and decide to give us a hand." Cinead stopped then and looked expectantly at Gregory.

Gregory shook his head and replied, "Cinead, my friend, you know we Templars are not allowed to get involved in such matters. We are to only concern ourselves with matters concerning the Holy Lands and pilgrims unless the Pope or the Grand Master decides God would have us take part."

Cinead's face turned nearly as red as his beard, and his voice rose in volume as he said, "Your burn is out the window! Last I heard, your Grand Master was in prison confessing to everything the Inquisition accuses him of. I hear he even repeated his confession to the University of Paris. From the sounds of it, the Pope has abandoned you as much as He's abandoned our King. You're off your head!"

Gregory said, "I'm sorry, Cinead. I have no orders that permit me to intervene in a clearly temporal matter, such as a border dispute. I will give you this to think about. Although some, and maybe most of us Templars who are here, with the forbearance of your King, will be leaving, I'm sure not all of us will leave. I've already been informed that several of our lay brothers, most of whom are not knights, but are squires and archers, desire to be released from their commitment to the Templars. Many wish to stay here in Scotland rather than risk returning to Paris. This should add to your numbers. Lastly, I would ask that you do not speak ill of our Grand Master. You don't understand what is going on in the dungeons of France any better than I understand a Bishop forgiving a man of murder on Holy ground."

Cinead looked about ready to strike Admiral Gregory, but slowly regained control and said, "This is no border dispute! Half-trained men are what you offer? After what we have done for you."

Gregory, attempting to show his sympathy, said, "Cinead, you have been a friend of mine for many years, and you know the Order I serve is strict. I will make sure you are generously compensated for what you and King Robert have done for us, but I cannot give you men who have sworn a life-long oath to God and our Order."

Cinead barked, as he abruptly turned and walked away, "Go boil your head. Don't want your money, we need your swords!"

Sir William, who was still in shock at the rapid rise of Cinead's anger, said, "What just happened? I thought you two were friends."

Gregory replied, "We are friends. Cinead, like many Scots, tends to get angry quickly. Add to that the fact that he is a patriot fighting for his country. He knows they need to deal with the Comyn situation quickly before King Edward II can stabilize things back in England and mount an expedition north, or Robert the Bruce will face Edward to the South and the Comyns to the North. We'll let Cinead calm down after a day or so, he'll punch me in the chest hard enough to take my breath away or slap me on the back hard enough I'll nearly fall on my face, and I'll know he's ok with me. What really has me concerned is I can't for the life of me figure out what 'your burn is out the window' means."

Chapter 21

Opening acts of the trial of the Knights Templar

The trials against the Templars started in Paris on October 19, 1307, just six days after the arrest. On October 24th the Grand Master, Jacques de Molay confessed that at his initiation into the Templars "The said receptor (Humbert of Pairaud-Master in England) caused a certain bronze cross to be brought into his presence, on which was the figure of the Crucified, and he said to him and ordered that he deny Christ whose image was there. He, although reluctant, did it; and then the same receptor ordered him to spit on it, but he spat on the floor. Asked how many times, he said on his oath that he did not spit, except once, and concerning this, he remembered well." Jacques de Molay denied charges of homosexuality and would say only that, "Nothing had been done to him that had not been done to others."

The following day, the Grand Master was brought before the University of Paris to repeat his confession openly. King Philip IV of France worked diligently, mostly through his agent Guillaume de Nogaret, to convince Pope Clement V and the other Monarchs of the guilt of the Knights Templar.

Initially, the Pope was outraged by the actions of the King of France against the Templars. On October 27th, the Pope wrote a letter to King Philip expressing his anger over the arrests. King Philip responded by stating that he only arrested the Templars after the head of the Inquisition in France (who was more a servant of Philip than the Church) told him of the actions of the Templars and informed the King that he must arrest these men for the good of Christendom. The King then sent records of the confessions of the Templars being "questioned" and accusations by others against the Templars. The weight of the confessions caused the Pope to waver in His support of the Templars. The Pope sent his own men to question the Templars, who were held prisoner by the King of France. On December 24, 1307, Jacques de Molay retracted his confession before a Cardinal of the Pope.

The methods used to extract confessions came under question. It was learned that many of the men used to interrogate the Templars by King Philip were his own and not those of the Holy Inquisition, and that some of the methods used were not those approved by the Church. The Pope also expresses indignation due to King Philip IV's control of the amount of information Pope Clement V had access to, and that the King of France restricted which prisoners the Pope's men could question.

The issue that created the most difficulty for the Pope to attempt to stop the trial against the Templars was public opinion. The information that King Philip released to the populace of France was calculated to cause the utmost revulsion and dread of the Templars and create a public opinion based on an emotional response to the accusations and disregard for the facts that were coming out during the trial. Although the confessions that were gleaned under torture were damning to the Templars, if one looked at the accusations against the Cathers and the Jews that the King and Guillaume de Nogaret previously used, one would see an amazing similarity. Almost as if the names of the accused in the documents were the only thing that was changed. The only proof that seemed to support the case against the Templars was accusations by individuals who had a grudge against the Order, or individuals with a close relationship with the King, or confessions given by confused men who had obviously been mistreated physically and emotionally.

It appeared, after a few months, that the Pope finally became convinced that King Philip's case against the Templars lacked any true evidence, but he had to be careful how he was to proceed, since public opinion, especially in France, was against the Knights Templar.

Chapter 22

Henry felt that they were making no progress. The group of fellow Templars was meeting on a regular basis, but it seemed that was all they were doing. They would gather in their secret room in the cool, dark basement and discuss further ways to communicate in secret. After a few weeks, they had amassed a truly impressive array of hand signals, words, phrases, and handshakes to pass messages to each other unobtrusively, but they had not added a single new member nor come up with any plans to attempt to clear the name of the Templars. It seemed to Henry that they had fallen into a rut and were getting nowhere. All the while, events outside their basement had progressed poorly for the Templars.

Henry felt in his bones that they must make some significant move soon, or matters would play out, and they would have no choice but to remain hidden within the Hospitallers' Order and meet secretly in the dark room only to discuss secret words.

At the next meeting, Henry interrupted Jules de Verbeul, who was describing how he attempted to approach a fellow previous-Templar to discover his feelings, but he kept being interrupted by others. Henry said, "I'm sorry, brother, but I am tired of playing at keeping secrets and hiding in this room. I understand that it is risky for us to expose ourselves as true Templars, but all this hiding and scheming is getting us nowhere. We need to act before the King has crushed us completely. The confession of our Grand Master has seemed to settle the matter for many people."

Father Anthony said, "I agree, Henry, but what can we do? There are only nine of us. If we go before the King, we will surely be arrested and returned to our cells, and we will never be heard from again. If we go to the Pope, I do not know for sure what will happen, but I fear no better treatment than we would expect from King Philip. We need evidence of the King manipulating the confessions or…"

At that moment, they were interrupted by three raps on the stonewall. This was the signal the lone sentry, who stood outside the room, gave to indicate that someone was approaching. The men in the room fell silent and listened. After a moment, they heard two voices, but they couldn't make out what was being said. Then they could hear the sound of the crates concealing the door being moved. The men in the room all looked about for something to use as a weapon, but there was nothing. The only weapon the group had was the sword (they had acquired from the Hospitaller armory) that the guard at the door had with him. When the door opened, Gabriel du Breze, the sentry, said, "It's okay. A fellow Templar has come to join us."

As the candlelight fell on the face of the new individual to enter the chamber, Henry de Creon said in a surprised voice, "Gerrard de Le Languedoc! How did you know where to find us?"

Chapter 23

Father Thomas directed his attention solely on Pope Clement V and said in a calm voice that belied his anxiety, "Your Holiness, Odo, the squire who killed himself, told me that the creature Baphomet was worshipped in various forms by the Templars. This skull was only one of the idols. I believe that the beard and the glowing, which I also witnessed, must have started to fade once the evil artifact was moved from its home among the Templars and kept on true Holy ground. I fear that by the time we got the item here, those properties had left the object since the powers of the evil creature could not withstand long under the power of Christ."

Pope Clement thought in silence for a moment and then said, "Have you brought any other of these idols you claim my Templars worshiped.?"

Father Thomas replied, "As yet, we have not located any others. I believe the Knights have hidden them before their arrest. This head was found in a cellar beneath the Paris commandery, where it appears to have been concealed. As I understand it, it is only due to the glow it put off that the searchers were able to locate it."

Pope Clement said, "So again, I have no proof of any wrongdoing by my Templars. The only evidence you provide is confessions that, for the most part, are far less damaging than the accusations the King of France has made against the Order and the word of several men of dubious character, including a man who committed suicide rather than appear before Me."

Father Thomas bowed his head as if in contrition and replied, "I am sorry Your Holiness. The evil that pervades this Order seems to have had time to weave its tendrils deep into the leadership and planned to hide from the Light of God. Odo was not afraid of meeting Your Holiness; he was overwhelmed by all that he had experienced within the Templar organization. He was fearful of the evil he witnessed. Odo told me of many things that happened, such evil and indecent things that I loathe to share them out loud."

Pope Clement said, "Were you not a Templar yourself, Father Thomas? Perhaps you can tell us of the evil you saw with your own eyes."

Father Thomas' voice took on an edge of firmness, bordering on anger, and said, "I requested to join the Order so that I could discover the truth about the Templars because the King of France, Philip IV, had received many evil reports on them which He could not bring himself to believe. He felt it was his Christian duty to examine the matter further. Obviously, I must not have played my part very convincingly, for I was never allowed to witness anything beyond pride and occasional drunkenness. I am afraid I'm not very good at subterfuge. I did make a friend of the young squire Odo, and when the scales were finally removed from his eyes, he selected me as his confidant."

One of the Cardinals asked, "Were the scales removed from Odo's eyes before or after he was tortured by the King's men?"

Father Thomas, in a calmer and more conciliatory tone, replied, "Odo was a squire; he was not subjected to any torture or even questioned until he decided to come forward with what he knew. Odo told me he was cared for quite well by the King's men, better than his regular accommodations as a Templar squire."

The Cardinal huffed and said, "This would be the first occasion that we have heard of anyone claiming the King's men treated Templars well."

Pope Clement sighed softly and said, "If it is secondhand testimony that we must hear, then so be it. Before you start, let me remind you, I do not condemn a man just because someone has accused him. There are too many people who seek revenge for some perceived slight or advantage. I will need proof beyond mere accusations. Now tell me of this creature, Baphomet, and the idols the Templars supposedly worshipped."

Before Brother Jaye could speak, Father Thomas replied, "According to Odo, the Templars worshipped Baphomet in several images. Beside the bearded, glowing skull, there was a two-faced head, with one face facing forward and the other rearward. Additionally, there was a carved wooden image of a man, and an image of a cat, possibly representing the skull of a cat. Baphomet is a creature of Hell, and he slowly worked his way into the Templar organization. The creature contrived to get the Templars to give up the Holy Lands so that the Muslims could retake and defile the Holy City, Jerusalem. Then Baphomet was going to take over the Templars one by one until he had the entire organization under his sway. He planned to utilize the wealth of the Templars and the military strength of these renowned warriors to disseminate the false teachings of this evil creature throughout all their commanderies.

"The creature believed that by the time they were discovered, the corruption would have been spread so far that it would have been impossible for the Church to stop them. Luckily, the King of France, Philip IV, a loyal servant of God, discovered the plot and brought the creature of Hell into the light and with it the falsehood of the Templars."

Brother Jaye worked hard to manage his anger at Father Thomas. He let no emotion show on his face, but behind his calm exterior, Brother Jaye was seething with rage. Not only had Father Thomas taken control of the meeting with the Holy Father, but much of what Father Thomas had just shared with the Pope had never been confided to him. He knew Father Thomas was only out to serve himself and that he was withholding some information so that he would still have some leverage to remain useful to the King and the Inquisition. However, this conversation made Brother Jaye appear weak and of little value to the Holy See.

The Pope sat silent for a moment and then asked, "Again, I ask you, Father, are you not a Templar? Did you take the sacred vows of the Order?"

Father Thomas lowered his eyes as he said in a clear voice, "Yes, Your Holiness, I have taken the vows of a Templar, and I have not forsaken those vows. The vows I made were holy and righteous, and I do not claim otherwise. Within the Order, the Leadership, including many of the knights and sergeants, have taken new, secret, and unholy vows. I have not forsaken the vows I made before God and man; I feel blameless of the corruption the Order has come to represent. I would say that it is those others of the Templar Order, the ones who worship evil in secret dark meetings, who are no longer true Templars. They have forsaken Christ, Christianity, The Church, and Yourself in favor of the evil servant of Hell, Baphomet."

Again, the Holy Father was silent for some time in thought, then he said, "My Cardinals will review the papers you have brought, and I will consider these troubling matters. You have given me much to think about and prayerfully consider. Perhaps there is some rot in the apple that we must cut out. I will see you both back here in two days. I believe we have prepared a place for you to sleep and pray."

Chapter 24

Mary awoke one morning to the sounds of shouts above deck. They had been at sea for several days and had made their way to the English Channel, where they stayed just close enough to the English coast to see land to their portside as they made their way North. Captain Timm had told Mary that they were traveling against the current, but with the wind nearly directly astern of the ship, they were making good headway.

As Mary made her way past the crates that Captain Timm had set up to work as makeshift walls in the hold of the ship to give her some privacy in the cramped surroundings, she ran into Father Lull. Mary asked the father, "What is going on, Father?"

Father Lull said, "I don't know. I was just going up to see for myself. Care to join me?"

Mary waved him ahead as an answer. As they arrived on deck, they noticed it was a beautiful sunny day; seagulls were gliding overhead, making their familiar caws. They then realized the sail was down and was being tied to the mainstay. And there wasn't a hint of a breeze in the air. Captain Timm was near the starboard rail, yelling across a short gap to one of the other ships in their small flotilla. Mary noticed Derrick was with a group of sailors who were lowering the small rowboat over the side of the Jocelyn (as Mary began to think of the ship, although she never said it out loud to anyone, including Derrick or Father Lull).

The ship alongside the Jocelyn started to move away under the power of oars that had been run out over her lower sides. Captain Timm turned and took in the flurry of activity, seeming satisfied. The captain then noticed Mary and Father Lull and motioned them to come to him.

Father Lull said, "What is happening, Captain? Has something gone wrong?"

Captain Timm said, "No, not really. During the night, the wind died, and with the current in this part of the channel flowing south, we began to drift backward. Since the water is shallow here, I ordered all three vessels to drop anchor until we got a favorable wind, but at first light, we noticed some ships to our port heading our way. I ordered the other two ships of our fleet to row East further into the channel until they reach the current that flows North, and then for the two of them to continue together to Germany. With our higher sideboard, we cannot row directly, so I have had the men lower the launch and attempt to tow us. Although I doubt they will be able to do much. I am considering turning our ship and using the current to angle her East, but I do not believe it will really benefit us much and would clearly indicate we are trying to evade the approaching ships, which would only increase the likelihood of them chasing us down. As it stands now, we are just three ships caught in the doldrums attempting to continue North as best that we can."

Mary looked West at the slowly approaching ships and asked, "What do you suppose they want?"

Captain Timm, following her gaze, said, "Probably nothing, they appear to be five in number and about our size. They probably just happen to be in the area, possibly on their way to France or Germany like us. But there are currently hostilities with Scotland, and with a new English King, they may be ordered to stop all vessels they see to determine their intentions. In any case, we pose no threat, but I'd rather they don't come aboard and get a look at our cargo."

After over an hour of the launch attempting to pull the much larger Jocelyn, it was clear it was useless. The only headway made was when the men on deck took in some of the slack on the anchor line, which pulled the vessel against the current. All on deck could now clearly see the ships to their West slowly drawing closer. There were no sails evident, so they must be using oars. As the ships grew closer, they could make out that they were English and that they were on an intercept course with the Jocelyn. Captain Timm started to grow more concerned. He was certain they would want to board and inspect his ship to make sure they weren't taking men or supplies to Scotland to aid Robert the Bruce in his rebellion. Momentarily, he regretted sending the other two ships away, but even three to five odds weren't very good, especially with no wind. This way, at least most of the Templar treasure would escape.

Mary interrupted his thoughts and asked Captain Timm, "Captain, how many anchors do you have?"

Captain Timm replied, "Three. Why do you ask?"

Mary said, "I was wondering, if you have enough anchor line, would it be possible to pull the ship eastward using the other anchor."

Captain looked at Mary quizzically and said, "What do you mean?"

Mary said, "Well, you said this portion of the Channel was shallow, so I thought possibly we could put one of the anchors in the launch with as much anchor line as possible. Have the men row the launch northeast as far as the line allows, drop the anchor. Then we haul up the other anchor and have the men on deck pull in the slack on the new anchor line and then repeat the process, thereby dragging our way to the Northbound current."

Father Lull looked from Mary to Captain Timm, "Would that work, Captain?"

Captain Timm was looking off thoughtfully to Starboard as he said, "I believe it might. We often do something similar in harbors, but I've never heard of anyone trying it in open water. I wonder if you are the first to think of this, Mary?"

Then Captain Timm recalled the launch and barked new orders. In a short time, Mary's wild plan became a reality, and Jocelyn slowly started to make her way East. Yet the English ships still gained on them.

Chapter 25

Admiral Gregory was starting to think he was wrong in assuming Cinead would forgive him for not leaving any of the sworn Templar Knights to aid the Scots in their war against England. He had only seen Cinead twice since that time. One time, it was just Cinead's back as he stomped away at a quick pace. The second time the two men were walking toward one another, when Cinead noticed Gregory, the color rose in Cinead's face, and he walked past Gregory without a word or a second glance.

Gregory knew better than to try to speak to Cinead; he would have to wait until the big man decided to forgive him if he ever did. At the time, Gregory had a great many tasks to keep him busy, so there was little time to dwell on how Cinead was feeling or acting. Admiral Gregory was having to organize the ships and men they had brought to Scotland to keep them out of King Philip's reach. He had over a thousand men here; about six hundred were sworn brothers. All but a few would need to be moved by ship to Bergen, Norway, and most of his ships could only carry about twenty passengers, plus a four- or five-man crew. He had enough ships to complete the task in one trip, but it still required careful planning to ensure the ships were in order, the food, water, and gear were stowed, and the men were all prepared to sail.

Some of the men, who were not sworn brothers but rather men who had pledged themselves to work with or for the Templars for a set duration, would come with them. Yet Gregory needed to get a better idea of the number of men who were choosing to stay here with the Scottish. Most of the men who would remain in Scotland were craftsmen and laborers, but there was a fair number of archers who the Templars hired since they did not train their own archers. The knights thought it unchivalrous to use a bow as a weapon of war. Like most military Orders, they did not allow archers to be sworn brothers, but realizing their value, they would hire archers for set periods of time. It was the squires who made up the largest unknown; they had not yet made any vows to the

Templars, but most had been with the Templars for many years and had intended to take monastic vows once they were knighted.

Admiral Gregory, along with three of his senior Captains, and Sir William were going over the supplies for each of the ships and the number of men he intended to have aboard each vessel for the continuation of their trip when Sir Jules des Morvan approached them.

Sir Jules said to Gregory, "Why have you canceled heraldry class without first speaking with me?"

Admiral Gregory was in no mood to be questioned by this man who thought much more of himself than he ought. Attempting to control his rising anger, Gregory said, "Sir Jules, I sent one of my squires to you this morning to inform you that I had need of every available man to begin the process of making the ships ready for the rapidly upcoming voyage. Did he not find you?"

Sir Jules said, "A young man tried to interrupt my preparations for the heraldry class, but I refused to see him since I was very busy and I felt if it was truly important a Knight would have been sent to me, not a boy, who by the way, has not darkened the door of a single one of my classes."

Admiral Gregory, who had been standing over a make-shift table, clenched his fists and stood up straighter and said sarcastically, "I am sorry to have bothered you. I'm sure it was very annoying to be interrupted while performing an important task by someone you hold little respect for."

Sir Jules, having not noticed the sarcasm, said, "Thank you, although I doubt you understand how important these classes are, or how much preparation goes into them. I will expect the students back as soon as you can deliver them." As Jules said this, he made to turn in order to leave.

Admiral Gregory said as he stepped away from the table, "Sir Jules, I believe I have not made myself clear. I realize that you have lived your life under the misconception that you are more important than others due to the family you come from, but that does not hold true here and now. Yet so that you will have the opportunity to teach your student what true brotherhood and loyalty are within our

Order, I will have one of the knights take you directly to your new classroom."

Sir Jules had a look of utter confusion on his face and was apparently lost by the turn in the conversation. Admiral Gregory said to one of the knights who was present just outside the tent, "Sir Hue, please escort Sir Jules to one of the ships and have one of the sailors instruct the good teacher on how to properly caulk a ship and kindly remain there to make sure he performs his lessons until Vespers."

Sir Jules' voice rose to a sharp edge as he said, "You cannot do this. I am Preceptor of Inverness, and my father is Lord…" That was as far as he got before Admiral Gregory struck him with an open hand on the left side of his face, nearly knocking him to the ground

Admiral Gregory said in a suddenly calmer voice, "I do not care who your father is. Now go do something useful."

Sir Hue took Jules by the arm and guided him quickly away before Jules could think of anything to say that might provoke another blow from the Admiral.

Admiral Gregory was somewhat ashamed by his outburst of anger and said to the rest of the men who had witnessed the event, "I am sorry, gentlemen, I should probably not have struck him. Yet, I have no patience for that elitist self-importance at a time when we need everyone to pull their own weight. If I could, I'd release Sir Jules from his vows to the Templars and the Church and leave his ass here in Scotland."

A voice boomed from behind him, "If you leave that popinjay here when you depart, I will never forgive you or welcome you back to my shores, no matter what or who might be chasing you."

Admiral Gregory turned to see Cinead standing there with a grin on his face. The two men shook hands, and Admiral Gregory said to the other Templars, "If you could give me a moment." And Cinead and Gregory stepped a few paces away to talk."

Sir William said to Louis, who was at the meeting to attend William, "I'm glad that's over."

Louis asked, "Which Admiral Gregory and Sir Jules, or Admiral Gregory and Cinead?" Before William could answer, Louis continued, "Can we talk for a moment?"

Sir William said, "Of course, at least until the Admiral is ready to resume."

Louis said, "I'm having a little trouble coming to a decision regarding whether I want to continue the voyage or remain here in Scotland."

Sir William was caught completely off guard by this comment. William was certain Louis still planned to take monastic vows and take the Templar mantle as soon as he was knighted. He and Louis had been working every day on their arms training. Louis had reached the point where William was no longer certain he could teach him much. Several of the Scottish knights who had grown fond of Louis often took him aside and showed him other facets of fighting on foot. It was soon discovered Louis had quite a knack for the pike. Louis even had the armorers modify the crosspiece, which was about two feet behind the tip of the spearhead. He suggested that if the cross piece had more of a hook shape, it could be used to dismount soldiers on horseback more easily, thereby making the weapon more useful against cavalry.

William asked Louis, "I don't understand. I thought you wanted to be a Templar?"

Louis replied, "I'm not sure what that even means now. There is no Crusade in the Holy Lands or any plans for one. There are no pilgrims to protect. With all that has happened over the last few months, I'm not even sure there are monastic vows that I can take. I need to understand what is happening with the Templars and what we are becoming. Where are we going? What is our purpose? Do we even have a purpose other than running from the various Catholic Monarchs and the Pope? If the Holy Father no longer recognizes us, does the Order even exist? Under whose authority do we act? Are we even Catholic? If not, what are we? There are too many questions without answers for me to make a commitment to the Templar Order in good conscience.

"I always saw myself as a champion of those who could not protect themselves. I have no desire to be a knight who spends all his time in court carrying out the orders of some local Lord, no matter how it affects the lives of regular people. I feel I need a calling, a true purpose that is greater than my petty wants and desires."

Williams, again surprised by the depth of thought Louis had put into things and a little angered because he felt Louis' remarks also implied he was not serving a real purpose, asked, "So, you want to stay in Scotland for what reason? Have you met a girl?"

Louis almost laughed and said, "No, I've met several girls, but that's not it. I honestly don't know what to do. That's why I'm talking to you. It would almost be easier if I had taken vows before all this. Then, like yourself, I would already have made a commitment and would be bound to the Templar Order. After all that has happened, I'm not sure if there is a reason to remain committed to an Order that appears to have lost its direction. Yet, at the same time, I don't know what to do. I'd always planned on being a Templar. I could take monastic vows and live out my life as a monk, but I don't feel that would be the direction I'd want to go."

William put his hand on Louis' shoulder and said, "Look, Louis, this has been stressful for all of us. We all must decide what is best for the Order, not just ourselves. I don't think running away is the answer. I think you should take the rest of the day and just be still and listen to God. I'm sure once you have thought it through, it will become clear that God wants you to continue your present path and become a brother Templar."

Louis was about to reply rather sharply to the condescending way William was talking to him, but just then, Admiral Gregory returned. William, still with his hand on Louis' shoulder, guided him to the exit and said, "I'll be fine here without you, Louis. Go."

As Louis stood outside the tent, uncertain what to do, he heard Sir William say to the others, "I must have been overworking the lad. He needs some time to get his priorities in order."

Chapter 26

Gerrard de Le Languedoc stood in the semi-darkness of the room and said, "It was not difficult to locate you. The members of this secret group have obviously been engaging in some activity, speaking in a manner that is only half-heard and making no sense, creating strange shapes with their hands, and then looking with anticipation as if they were waiting for a response. All the former Templars know you are up to something, but most just want to ignore you, hoping you'll tire of these games and get on with being a novice Hospitaller."

Father Anthony asked, "How did you discover when and where we were meeting?"

Gerrard said, "Again, that was easy. I noticed an increase in the number of members of your group whispering among yourselves, and I simply watched and listened. When I saw Jules de Verneuil slip out of his cell, I followed. Now, I have a question for you. What do you hope to accomplish with all this sneaking about?"

Henry was embarrassed by being so easily discovered and by the fact that a man he respected thought that this skullduggery was little more than an adolescent game.

Father Anthony answered, "We are hoping to restore the good name of the Knights Templar. A goal I would think any loyal Templar would have."

Gerrard asked, "How do you wish to accomplish this task? Don't you see everything that is stacked against a mission of that nature? The King of France is actively trying to convince the other Monarchs of Europe of our guilt. A great many of our brothers and almost all our leadership have confessed to crimes that must be punished, and no less punishment than the complete destruction of our Order seems appropriate. The Pope seems to waver between one position and another. He is placed in a situation where standing up for us would mean stating that the methods of the Inquisition are unjust and unrighteous, bringing into question past instances where the same methods were used to root out evil.

"Additionally, the Pope must consider public opinion, which is so strong against us. It surprises me that there hasn't been a mob calling for the head of Grand Master Jacques de Molay. What do you suppose you can do against all this as novice monks hiding in a sub-basement?"

No one spoke for a moment, then Sir Henry said, "Sir Gerrard, we have no firm plans as yet. That is why we are meeting to determine what, if anything, can be done."

Again, there was a pause before Sir Gerrard said, "What we need to do is remind the people of France of the honor and past glory of our Order and to remind the King that not all of us have been broken by his tortures, that we remain a force to be dealt with."

Father Anthony said, "I may have an idea. I have been thinking about it, but I was trying to come up with a complete plan before presenting anything; perhaps now is the time. The other day, several crates were delivered here from the Templar commandery that contained items from our former armory. Being that there are so few Hospitallers here, the crates were placed in storage for now until they can be sent where they are needed."

Henry asked, "What type of items are we talking about, Father? And how would items from our commandery help establish our innocence?"

Father Anthony replied, "I'm not certain of what is in all the crates, but I know there are Templar mantles and caparisons for Templar war horses. What effect on the citizenry and the political leaders do you think there would be if, say, ten Knights Templar in full regalia came riding up to the castle gates demanding to be allowed to respond to the false charges brought against us?"

Chapter 27

Pope Clement V sat quietly in his chair as the Cardinals tried to convince him to continue to oppose King Philip IV of France in his attack on the Templars. The Pope had initially been outraged by the actions of the King, and the Holy Father had spoken out against King Philip when word of the arrest had reached him. Then the confessions started pouring in. Confessions extracted by members of the Inquisition and, therefore, beyond reproach. Even though the Pope and the College of Cardinals were aware that something like this was in the works, the reach and severity of the action taken by King Philip against the Templars were still shocking when it occurred.

Pope Clement found himself in a very difficult situation. The people of France had heard about the confessions and their nature. Worse yet, the people of France believed the charges and seemed to take delight in the downfall of the Templars; thus, if he stood up against Philip, it would likely incite the people of France against him.

The Holy Father was only half listening when he caught the end of a suggestion by one of the Cardinals. The Cardinal, DeAngelo, was saying, "Perhaps the Swiss Confederacy would be a good location."

Pope Clement asked, "I beg your pardon, I was trying to process my thoughts and wasn't paying proper attention. What would make Switzerland a good location for?"

Cardinal DeAngelo replied, "No need to apologize, Your Holiness, we are all aware of the pressures you are under, and we are here only to serve as you see fit. I was just thinking that perhaps we could request more of the Templars held by the King to be sent here for further questioning, and instead of sending them back to King Philip as we previously did, we could send them to the Swiss Confederacy. It is close by, and with it being a new government establishment, I believe the Templars could stay there out of the reach of the French Crown, and perhaps they would allow the

Templars to establish themselves there as a base of operation until this issue can be resolved."

The Holy Father thought to himself that this may be a good idea; he would need to pray on this further, but now…, "We will need to return to this later. We need to receive Father Thomas and Brother Jaye soon, and I would appreciate your recommendations on what to say to them. I believe you have all read through the documents that they brought with them from the French King and Guillaume de Nogaret."

The Cardinals were all silent for a moment, waiting for someone to start. Finally, Cardinal Emmerata said, "I have read through the confessions, they are all nearly the same and at first I thought perhaps there is some truth to it since they are all so similar but then it started to look as though those confessions were made by men who were just repeating words that had been put in their mouth. The crimes are mostly denying Christ in some ritual during a secret meeting, many times involving spitting on or near the cross. There are also some confessions of various acts of homosexuality. There are confessions regarding an image or idol that is worshiped or venerated, and a few do mention a creature named Baphomet. The more I read it, the more the words sounded like those of Guillaume de Nogaret and less like those of penitent men seeking absolution for their sins."

Pope Clement asked, "What about the rest of you?" There was general agreement among the rest of those present.

The Holy Father then asked, "What do you gentlemen think we should say to the King's envoys? And what do you think of this Baphomet? Is this creature real or another nail the King wishes to use to seal His case against the Templars? I do not like this talk of a creature of Hell with designs on the Holy Roman Church. Could there be any truth to this? I am certain that Brother Jaye is more a servant of the King than he is a servant of the Church, but Father Thomas may be what he claims."

Again, there was a brief pause while the Cardinals waited for one of their numbers to speak up. Cardinal Hughes finally said, "I am inclined to agree with Your assessment, Holy Father, on Brother

Jaye, but I believe Father Thomas is a servant of Father Thomas. I believe he will say or do whatever is in his own best interest."

Another Cardinal, Cardinal Soprano, said, "Perhaps we can use that."

Cardinal Hughes asked, "How can we use that? We cannot use deception to bring the Truth to light."

Cardinal Soprano said, "Perhaps we can help Father Thomas understand that his own best interest lies with us rather than a King who has been dealing so treacherously with anyone who stands in his way or knows secrets he is trying to keep. This King seems to feel he is semi-divine and that his position as King of France places him above the Throne of Saint Peter, and Father Thomas has come to believe this lie. Perhaps we can show Father Thomas the error of his way.'

Pope Clement added, as if in thought, "Perhaps saving Father Thomas's soul in the process."

Chapter 28

After several hours of dragging the ship, yard by yard, eastward using Mary's idea, Captain Timm realized there was no way they could reach the northward current before the five ships would reach them. He called the launch back and had most of the men go below deck to try and conceal the cargo as best they could. He also preferred to have as many men out of sight as possible in case they were boarded; it probably wouldn't matter much with the odds they would face in such a situation, but every little bit helps.

As the ships grew closer, it was clear they were English as they flew a white flag with a red Saint George's cross. Three of them were Hulks of similar design to the two Captain Timm had commanded to continue to Germany. The other two were smaller and appeared to be large rowboats, probably fishing vessels pressed into service to protect the coast. Captain Timm noted several men in the fore and aft castles armed with crossbows. The two rowboats, being lighter and faster, reach the Jocelyn first. They rowed to the East side of the Jocelyn and took up station there.

Captain Timm also noted that off to the South, a squall was developing and thought that if he just had another thirty minutes, or maybe less, the storm might have provided the wind his ship needed. Nothing he could do about that now. Mary, Derrick, and Father Lull Had joined the captain near the helm. One of the Hulks, nearly as large as the Jocelyn, rowed up along the port side so close that one would not have to yell to be heard talking to those on the other ship. A man wearing a full chainmail hauberk, but oddly, on his head, he wore what appeared to be a large-brimmed farmer's hat with a peacock feather protruding from it. The man removed his hat and made a sweeping motion downward with it and bowed. As he placed the strange hat back on his head, in a cultured English voice, the man yelled to them, "I am Sir Archibald, servant of Edward II, King of England. And you gentlemen, and lady, might be?"

Captain Timm said, "Pleased to meet you, Sir Archibald. I am Captain Timm, and my friends are Father Lull, Derrick, and Lady Mary. May we be of any assistance?"

Sir Archibald replied, "I was going to ask you the same. It appears your two companions have abandoned you, as we saw them row away as we approached."

Captain Timm, still sounding calm and friendly, said, "They merely continued on with their voyage. You know how it is with us merchant ships. We join in small flotillas when it benefits us all, but if a ship slows us down, we just as quickly part company."

The feather on Sir Archibald's hat fluttered momentarily in front of his face so that he swiped it away with the back of his hand and said, "Ah, so you are a merchant. Where are you headed? As I can see, you are quite low in the water and must have cargo aboard. You wish to trade. Perhaps you have something my King would be interested in, arms? Armor? Soldiers?"

Captain Timm laughed and said, "Nothing so interesting, we are coming from Greece. We have olives and olive oil. We are making our way North to Germany."

Sir Archibald said, "I do love good olives; perhaps I can come aboard, and we can work out a mutually agreeable trade so that you won't have to go visit those Germans."

Captain Timm said, "That would be nice, but I'm afraid I already have a buyer who is waiting on this cargo."

Sir Archibald was growing tired of this game, and the feather again fluttered in front of his face, causing him to remove the hat in irritation. He said in a less jovial tone, "I'm afraid I must insist. I need to inspect your cargo and ensure you are not transporting goods to the Scots. I expect you to accommodate us." All three of the larger ships started lowering small boats over their side, and men, some soldiers, some sailors, began clambering over the side.

As this was happening, Captain Timm made some hand gestures to his first mate, who had five men remaining on deck, to move to the yardarm. Just as Sir Archibald was about to follow his men over the side to get in the boat, the ship he was on was rolled by a wave, and the hat he had just returned to the top of his head to free his hands so he could climb down flew off his head in a gust of wind. Sir Archibald, obviously not at home at sea, reached for the hat, lost his grip on the side of the ship, and fell, disappearing into the darkening water. The squall hit them all at that moment with a torrent of rain, six to eight-foot seas, and strong winds. Sir Archibald was dragged beneath the waters by his heavy hauberk.

Captain Timm shouted an order to the men standing ready by the yardarm. They hoisted the sail, which filled with the rapidly increasing wind and snapped too in a resounding boom. The first mate ran forward with an ax and cut the line to the anchor. The Jocelyn lurched forward by the strong wind, and Captain Timm turned the wheel hard over to starboard, bearing down on the two rowboats, which scrambled to get out of the way of the much larger vessel. A few crossbow bolts were loosed by the men stationed on the castles of the English ships, but in the suddenly rough seas and the rapid acceleration of the Jocelyn, most flew harmlessly off-target, most but not all. The Jocelyn moved rapidly in the strong wind away from the English, who were still trying to raise the sail. The Jocelyn was soon lost from sight in the squall.

Mary was the first to notice that Captain Timm had been hit by a crossbow bolt. The bolt had gone through his neck from left to right. He must have died very quickly, as his hands still grasped the wheel. Derrick and Father Lull unclenched their hands from the helm and laid him down on the deck. Mary had taken the wheel while they did this, until the first mate, Raphael, arrived and found Captain Timm dead. He instantly barked orders to some of the men who disappeared below deck, and then the first mate took over the helm from Mary. Father Lull performed Last Rites over the body of the fallen Captain as the ship was driven east by the raging storm.

Chapter 29

Louis decided to take the rest of the day off, as Sir William had instructed him to. He gathered a few supplies, including some cheese and bread, and started walking. He left Inverness behind and went off into the countryside. Speaking with Sir William had been a waste of time. Louis liked Sir William and respected him as a leader, but William was not an individual who attempted to look at things from other viewpoints. He wasn't close-minded, just focused on the task at hand, and fully committed to the Templar Order.

Louis supposed he should have known better. William had a family history grounded in the Templars; he shouldn't have expected William to understand his questioning the very nature of the Order. To Louis, it seemed the Templars stood on a precipice that would lead to great change or destruction.

Louis was willing to die for the Templars, as they were warrior monks committed to protecting pilgrims who traveled to the Holy Land. Soldiers who are committed to guarding and defending the holy sites of Israel. He had dreamed of walking the streets where Jesus' feet had trodden, to reclaim and hold the city of Jerusalem from the Muslims, to inhabit the Temple of Solomon, their original headquarters. He just didn't feel the same calling when he thought of joining an Order of warrior/monks whose fight now seems to be that of hiding from the head of every church he would make vows to serve. How did that make any sense? When he thought about it, he didn't really understand how he could become a Templar. Can you make a vow to someone if they refuse to accept it? He supposed in some instances you could, but in this case, he didn't see how it would be valid. He could perhaps make a vow to the Templar Order, but it could not be the same as the monastic vows all the Templars had made before this craziness started.

Louis was raised a Catholic, and even though he was somewhat rebellious, he loved the church deeply in his soul. When he thought of that feeling that often overcame him during Mass, it nearly brought tears to his eyes. He wanted to be part of something that sought to pursue a deeper understanding of God and had at its heart a goal to help others. He wanted to be a Templar of old, riding into battle to protect Christians, unconcerned about whether he lived or died, because he knew he was fighting as a soldier of God, but that did not appear to be in the Templars' future any longer.

He knew the charges against the Templars were false, but it didn't seem to matter. Those with more power had seized control of public opinion, and the other powers who had the ability to sway things in favor of the Templars appeared to be silent. Admiral Gregory had informed him that the Templars in Portugal were being received as welcome warriors of the Church by King Dinis, and they and their possessions were under the protection of the King of Portugal. Perhaps he could go there, but no, Portugal is not the Holy Lands.

Louis had been walking for about three hours by now, and he suddenly stopped and looked around. The beauty of Scotland suddenly overcame him. The fields around him were green with patches of blue and violet wildflowers. The day was overcast, and the clouds seemed low and heavy as if ready to rain, but so far, there was only a light mist falling. Up ahead Louis saw one of the many peaks that seemed to thrust up out of the fertile green ground. About halfway up the peak, it was green with growth and then suddenly, the green stopped, and bare rock seemed to burst through the lush foliage. It was a contrast that seemed to typify this wonderful country. He looked about himself and knew why these people felt such a connection with the land and were so committed to making it theirs again.

Louis thought maybe he should stay here and fight with the Scots. He could easily love this land and these people. There was something of a kindred spirit he felt with them. As he pondered these thoughts, he continued to walk and found himself climbing up the peak in front of him. The exertion did him good; it kept him moving and working, and his troubled thoughts drifted as he focused on just placing one foot in front of the other to keep climbing. Faster and faster, he climbed until he was covered in sweat, and his breath came in the familiar steady rhythm of deep inhalation and exhalation that he also experienced during martial training. He reached the point where the green gave way to barren rock and came to a stop. He seated himself on the ground and just looked out before him.

As he sat there slowing his breathing and gazing at the wild countryside, he knew he could not stay. This was also not his calling, but what was? Louis called out to God in a heart heavy with anguish and uncertainty. He looked at the clouds above his head so close he could almost touch them and cried out, "Lord Father, what am I to do? I want to believe, to be committed to... something. I want to know what to do, where to go. All that I have trained to do, everything I had planned for, has been crushed." Tears welled up in his eyes, and his throat grew tight. His voice grew louder, and he yelled in anger, "God, it feels as though everything is being torn from me. It seems like there are far more questions than answers. I may not have been the best Catholic, but I always trusted in the Church, the Virgin Mary, the saints, and Christ, but now it appears the Church is turned against me. Please help me. I know I'm only one squire in this whole wide world, but I want to be more, even if no one knows but myself. I don't want glory; I want the peace to know I'm doing the right thing."

Louis lowered his head, closed his eyes, and waited, hoping for an answer. He wanted a voice to speak out to him, to tell him what to do. As time passed, he heard the wind rustle through the grass, the far-off rumble of thunder, but no voice. He felt the temperature drop, which made him shiver in his sweat-damp clothes. He regained control, which was oddly discomforting. He wanted that disconcerting feeling that came when he exposed himself before God to return, but it had passed. Then he heard something. He realized he had been hearing it for a while but hadn't noticed until now - it was the baaing of sheep. He opened his eyes and looked around. Down below him were sheep chewing on grass. One was not more than twenty feet in front of him, looking dumbly up at him while it chewed. A female voice behind him said, "So, did God answer ya?"

Louis jumped up and spun around. There, sitting not far behind him, was a lass from Inverness that he had seen many times, but never spoken to; her name was Isla. She was tall with long hair, more blond than red. She always wore loose, heavy clothing that appeared to be an attempt to conceal her figure, but upon closer inspection, one could tell she was very pleasantly curved. She didn't seem inclined to laughter and childish games like most of the young Scottish women Louis met. She had a stern take-charge manner that kept everyone around her in line and on task. Louis gaped at her, wondering how she crept up on him and how long she had been there.

Isla, noting the concerned expression on his face, said, "Don't be worried. I didn't hear your confession or anything. I could just tell that you were praying, by the way you sat there, all quiet with your eyes closed, as if you expected God to drop an answer from the heavens. Did you get the answer ya wanted?"

Louis relaxed a bit and said, "Uhm, no. No answer, but I think you scared three years off my life. How did you sneak up on me?"

Isla said, "It wasn't hard; you were focused on your praying. By the way, I didn't sneak up on you. I just walked over and sat down to keep an eye on my sheep."

Louis asked, "This seems quite a way out from town to feed sheep."

Isla replied, "Yes, I should start heading back. I sometimes like to wander further out just to get a look at something different."

She stood and started walking down the slope back toward the town. Louis got up and followed, soon catching up with her. He asked, "Don't you need to herd the sheep up and guide them back to the village?"

Isla gave him a side glance and laughed, "You don't know much about sheep, do ya? Sheep are the stupidest animals on God's earth. Once they have a leader, they will follow them off a cliff. I'm their leader. I only need to watch for stragglers who might not be paying attention and not notice we've all left. You know the Father in our Church says God says we are like sheep; do you suppose that means we're stupid?"

Louis laughed and said, "Perhaps it does. Or maybe it means we are followers. Or should be followers. I don't know."

They walked in silence a while, and then Isla said, "Here's another stupid thing about sheep; they won't drink from water that is moving very fast. If it's a slow-moving stream that's not making much noise, they'll drink, but if the water is splashing about even a little, they'll die of thirst, staring at the water rather than drinking. I often have to dig out a small pond area along a faster-moving stream to water the sheep. Now, how stupid is that? But at least they're not goats."

"What's wrong with goats?" Louis asked.

"Well, sheep are stupid, but goats are just sheep with an attitude," Isla replied.

Chapter 30

It took almost two weeks to finalize everything. In the end, it proved not to be as difficult as they feared getting all the supplies for their little display moved to a stable adjacent to the Hospitaller's commandery. It seemed that no one within the Hospitallers' organization considered the former Templars to be in need of close watching. In fact, the former Templars soon discovered that if they completed all their tasks in a satisfactory manner, no one paid any attention to them at all. So as long as the practice yard was raked, the night soil pots were emptied, the armor was rust-free, and the kitchen pots scrubbed, no one asked anything about a couple of servants moving a crate from one Hospitaller building to another.

About three hours before Matins was to begin, Henry de Creon, Gabriel du Breze, Louis d'Aubigne, Victor de Lorraine, Jules de Verneuil, Gaspard de Troyes, Peter de Rhone, Father Anthony, Jamison the master mason, and Garrard de La Languedoc, made their way quietly to the Hospitaller stables. The men cloaked the horses, which they had borrowed from the Hospitallers, in a Templar caparison and then saddled them. They each then donned a chain mail hauberk and coif, and over this, they put a white surcoat emblazoned with the red Templar cross, and belted on a sword. The eight former Templar knights in the group felt at home in armor, but Father Anthony and Jamison the mason felt very weighed down. Father Anthony originally argued that he should come along dressed as the priest he was, but this was rejected because they felt that they needed to be wearing helmets to hide their individual identities. They wanted to appear to onlookers as Templars of old, coming to demand justice, rather than worn-down men complaining of injustice. They wrapped the horse's hooves in cloth to muffle the sounds of their hoof falls. Then they led their mounts out into the Paris streets.

The procession made its way to a warehouse area they believed would be quiet at this hour and waited until just before sunup. Then they removed the cloth from the horse's hooves, placed their helmets on their heads, and climbed into the saddle of their horses after helping Father Anthony and Jamison onto their horses. They rode at a slow pace, Henry de Creon leading the way by himself as their elected spokesman. The rest followed in three rows of three abreast.

The sunlight started to burn off the early morning fog as they made their way down the waking street. Those who saw them would not forget the sight which they related with awed excitement to everyone they spoke with for weeks afterward. Out of the shrouding fog, they would first hear the clopping of several horses approaching at a walk. Then, materializing as if out of a dream, came a horse and rider dressed in white, with a red cross pattee prominently displayed on the rider's chest and the horse's flanks. None of the riders spoke or looked to the side; they looked straight ahead, intent on their silent mission. Then they slowly disappeared into the swirling fog. They typically left the viewer feeling as if they had just witnessed something sacred, holy, and a bit otherworldly.

The ten riders made their way to the front gates of the Louvre fortress, where they believed King Philip to be. The nine riders behind Sir Henry fanned out in a line behind him and waited. They didn't have to wait long. The sun had completely burned off the morning fog, and the spectacle of ten Knights Templar in full regalia, when everyone believed they had all been arrested by the King, brought a rapid response from the King's men. Crossbowmen soon appeared on the wall above them, and a contingent of spearmen arrived at the gate. The spearmen parted, and a knight on horseback rode through their ranks. As the knight made his way toward the Templars, the spearmen followed behind him. The Templars sat silently, waiting, the only movement the swishing of the warhorse's tails. The knight who approached the Templars did not wear a helmet, either forgotten in his haste or more likely to show that he was not afraid of these men. Yet the look on his face could not hide the fact that he was clearly unnerved by the appearance of these Templars before him. The knight said, "I am Sir Renard of His Majesty King Philip IV of France. May I know who you men are and what you are doing here?"

Henry replied, "I'm one of many Poor Fellow Soldiers of Christ and of the Temple of Solomon, who have not fallen into the trap that King Philip IV set for myself and my brothers."

Sir Renard raised his hand in the traditional greeting, showing he had no weapon in his hands, and said in a somewhat shaken voice, "Brother knight, why have you come here?"

Henry did not return the raised hand and said in a voice seething with anger, "I am here to hear from the King's own lips why He has unlawfully arrested my true brothers and continues to hold them against the laws established by the Holy Roman Church."

During this exchange, the Parisian populace had slowly begun to creep out and move closer to see and hear what was happening.

Sir Renard tried to swallow, but his mouth had suddenly gone dry. He said, "I am sorry to disappoint you, but the King is not in Paris at this time. Perhaps you can come back later. I'm sure the King will be back in a week; you may call on Him then."

Henry de Creon wrapped the rains around his left fist one time and leaned forward just a bit as he replied, "I see. I recall a time not long ago when King Philip the Fair hid out in our Templar commandery for a few days, as the people of France wished to harm his royal head. He hid because he had decided to remove almost all the silver from the French coin, so that he could afford his lavish lifestyle, and didn't seem to care that it impoverished the people of France. I believe at that time He had his men tell those who wished him to explain his actions that he was not present at the commandery so that he could eat and drink uninterrupted."

More Parisians were gathering around the Templars. Henry did not seem to notice, but the other Templars certainly did. At first, they were concerned the crowd might attack them. It soon became clear that something had shifted in the feelings of those present; perhaps it was Henry reminding them of the wrongs perpetrated by their King in the past, or perhaps it was the sight of these ten men standing against the tyranny of the monarchy.

Henry continued, "Just over a year ago, he again found himself in financial ruin due to his overspending on luxuries, and what does our King do? He runs all the Jews out of France since He borrowed heavily from them and used this as His method to get out of paying back the money He had been loaned. Furthermore, our King took it upon himself to collect all debts owed to the Jewish moneylenders, as it wouldn't be a good idea to let the citizenry believe they didn't have to repay their debts. So, the King sent out his men to brutalize anyone who did not pay immediately. Again, when the people of France cried out for justice, the King could not be found.

"Then just a few months ago, The Iron King, Philip IV, along with his right-hand advisor, Guillaume de Nogaret, arrested and charged us Templars with a list of evil deeds that is laughable for anyone who knows of the Templar Rule and what we have forsaken to serve our God. The King has His men torture those arrested to get them to confess to crimes they never committed, or things they never even thought of. I was one of those men tortured, and so are these nine behind me, although, by the Grace of God, none of us broke under the pain and torment many of our poor brothers did. Our brothers, who were forced to confess to the falsehoods the King pressed on them, will have to account to God for their dishonesty in their time of trial, but I believe our God will be merciful…to them. Our God has witnessed the noble deeds of the Knights Templar, past and present, and knows the hearts of the men your King brutalized, forcing them to say untruths. Our God knows the deceitful, corrupt heart of King Philip IV, and I call him to account for his deeds. I call for the King of France to come out of hiding and answer for his deceit!"

Henry, who in his rage had not noticed the crowd of Parisians who had gathered around them, now heard a rumbling, low growling sound that erupted into an almost animalistic shout, repeatedly saying, "BRING OUT THE KING." The king's knight, who had been watching the crowd grow with alarming speed, glanced around in a panic, then he turned his horse around and galloped back through the gate with the spearmen, first scrambling out of the way of his horse and then rapidly trailing him. The gate was then closed and secured.

Sir Gerrard carefully moved his horse through the crowd so that he was beside Henry and said, "It may be time for us to depart. The King, if he is here, will clearly not show himself and the men on the walls will not likely loose a crossbow bolt while this crowd is around, but eventually, they will have to do something to disperse the crowd, and many will be hurt or killed, which will destroy the value of our stand here today. You spoke well, but a mob of people can become a problem for our cause as much as they are an asset at present. If we leave now in slow procession, I believe the crowd will follow for a while and then return to their daily tasks, but this will be remembered, and we will have struck a blow. Maybe a small blow, but wars have been won with a less auspicious start than this.

Henry made no reply but slowly began to turn his horse and make his way through the throng of people still shouting for the King to show himself. The nine other Templars closed in behind him as they slowly made their way through the crowd. The mob, as if cued by the slowly departing line of Knights Templar, grew strangely quiet as if they were witnessing a funeral procession. Henry could feel the weight of all the eyes upon him; he, like those following him, sat erect in the saddle and looked straight ahead.

Somewhere amid the crowd, a chant started. Henry couldn't tell what was being said at first, but slowly, as more voices took up the chant, he heard, "Militum Christi! Militum Christi! Militum Christi!" This was a common shout Templars yelled as they rode into battle. It was Latin for "Army of Christ!" This crowd of onlookers still believed in them, at least for the moment, and that faith washed over Henry in an unexpected wave, causing his eyes to fill with tears. He started to repeat under his breath one of the quotes by Saint Bernard de Clairvaux, who wrote the Templar Rule in 1128, a quote all Templars learned:

I am a witness to the Lamb,
Templar is truly a fearless knight, and secure on every side,
For his soul is protected by the armor of faith,
Just as his body is protected by the armor of steel,
He is thus doubly armed and needs fear neither demons nor men.

The line of Templars began to wind its way through the streets that surrounded the Louvre fortress. The crowd, just as Sir Gerrard had said, slowly dispersed back to their daily tasks. And the Knights made their way back toward the Hospitaller commandery. Each of them knew they would likely be arrested upon their return to the Hospitaller stronghold. There was no way to hide the fact that they had left without permission, and since everyone would soon know what they had done, the Hospitaller command would be forced to return them to the King's prisons. They didn't know what they would be tried for; they were not relapsed heretics since none of them had ever confessed to any of the crimes leveled against the Templars. When this was discussed ahead of time, Victor de Lorraine said that he thought it likely they would be charged with treason, which carried the penalty of being drawn and quartered. Henry, for one, felt being drawn and quartered might be the only death worse than being burned alive at the stake, which was the punishment a relapsed heretic received.

Suddenly, Henry stopped his horse as a Priest stepped in front of him with his hand raised. It was a moment before the priest caught his breath enough so that he could speak. Obviously, the priest had been running. When he finally caught his breath, he said, "You men need to come with me now. You will need to dismount and abandon your horses."

Henry asked the priest, "Who are you, and why must we come with you?"

The priest said, "Who I am is of no importance. The man who sent me wishes to help you, but you must come with me now."

Sir Henry de Creon made the decision in that instant. He turned and commanded everyone to dismount and remove their surcoat, which they were to leave here in the street with their horses and follow him. The Priest turned and began to move at a quick pace, followed by the ten men in armor.

Chapter 31

Brother Jaye and Father Thomas sat in the antechamber, waiting for their audience with the Pope. They both sat silently, neither looked at the other. Brother Jaye was still furious about the skull the foolish carpenter had cleaned, which rendered it just another unremarkable skull. He also realized that it was his fault for not inspecting the skull after allowing the carpenter to use it to make the box. Adding to Brother Jaye's anger was Father Thomas, who seemed to turn the whole fiasco of the skull to his advantage. Brother Jaye was no longer inclined to believe that his and Father Thomas's goals were in line with each other. The more Brother Jaye dwelled on the previous meeting with the Pope, the more he was inclined to make sure Father Thomas met with an untimely and gruesome end. Perhaps he could somehow arrange things so Thomas could be convicted of treason.

Thomas knew that he had crossed a line with Brother Jaye and was concerned as to how it was going to turn out. Brother Jaye was not someone he wanted to have against him, but he had come to realize that Brother Jaye was more a tool of others to wield than he was a force unto himself. He knew that as things stood now, Brother Jaye could hurt him, but if he could get an ally with more power, Brother Jaye would not be able to touch him.

Amid all this silent scheming, one of the Priests who served the College of Cardinals and the Pope stepped into the antechamber and said, "Gentleman, I am sorry you have waited so long. I have been asked to tell you, Brother Jaye, that the Holy Father appreciates your diligence in this matter, and they have reviewed all the papers you have delivered to the Holy See. You are free to go." Before Brother Jaye could make a reply, the Pope's messenger continued, "Father Thomas, Cardinal Soprano would like to meet you in the library. You can follow me."

Brother Jaye said, "Should I wait for Father Thomas? I believe the King expected him and me to return together."

The Priest said, "No, you may leave now. Father Thomas is not a servant of the King; he is a servant of God and the Holy Father,

Pope Clement V, just as you are. The Pope needs Father Thomas here. You are needed elsewhere." Then the Priest led Father Thomas out of the antechamber, as Brother Jaye glared angrily at their departing forms.

Father Thomas was unsure whether he liked this new development or not. He had no idea what the College of Cardinals wanted with him that required him to be separated from Brother Jaye. He feared that because Brother Jaye was known to have a clear connection with the King of France, the Cardinals might feel they should not harass Brother Jaye, but he was of little consequence, and no one would miss him. Possibly the Cardinals felt they could do as they wished with him. He just didn't know what this meeting with Cardinal Soprano might be. Nor did he know anything about Cardinal Soprano.

Father Thomas was led to a room that was clearly used by the Cardinals for study. There were numerous small wooden tables with chairs around the room and shelves that contained scrolls. The only man in the room was a Cardinal. He appeared to be in his sixties, was well-tanned, and was either very stout or slightly overweight; it was hard to tell due to the Cardinal's robes. He rose from his chair as Thomas entered and stepped forward to greet him. As Thomas was about to kneel and kiss the man's ring. The Cardinal waved him to stop and said, "Let's skip that foolishness, it's just the two of us here, and my ring needs no more kissing. I am Cardinal Soprano, and you are Father Thomas. I would like to speak with you privately about this whole shameful situation with the Templars."

Father Thomas was not put at ease by the informal attitude of the Cardinal; on the contrary, he was more cautious, and his guard went up even higher than normal. Thomas smiled and bowed his head slightly and said, "I am pleased to meet you, your eminence. I will gladly provide any help that I can."

Cardinal Soprano said, "While we meet here, you can call me Michael. And if you don't mind, I will call you Thomas. I wish for us to speak freely and openly. I'm afraid titles will only get in the way. Shall we sit?"

They both sat at a table with chairs catty-corner to each other. Cardinal Soprano said, "I heard what you said when you spoke to the Holy Father, and I have a few questions for you. To start with, I understand you were sent to work for the Templars as a spy for Guillaume de Nogaret under the pretense that you would aid the Templars as a legal advisor?"

Thomas replied, "I was not sent as a spy; I was sent because the Grand Master, Jacques de Molay, requested assistance in some legal matters. I served as a member of Guillaume de Nogaret's advisory council for approximately two years. When the request from the Grand Master was made, Guillaume de Nogaret felt that a priest might be the best choice, given that there would likely be ecclesiastical considerations. Before I left, Guillaume de Nogaret came to me and asked me to keep alert to any improprieties I witnessed. He then told me about the accusations that had been made to the King by two men who had served with the Templars."

Cardinal Soprano said, "Ah, yes, the former prior of Montfaucon, whom the Grand Master had imprisoned for his lascivious lifestyle and his open statements of outright heresy. The other is a man he met in prison, also sent there by the Templar Order, who, after taking the Templar mantle, was said to be filled with every vice and displayed no desire to follow the Rule he had sworn to obey. So, you have two men, both Templars, who were being punished by the Order for living corrupt lives and who had every motivation to lie to get freed. Not entirely credible witnesses, wouldn't you say?

"You say you were not a spy, but you were sent to surreptitiously observe the Templars and report back to the Crown what you saw and heard. I'm not certain there is a difference, but I shall not belabor the point; let us continue. What things did you report?"

Thomas replied, "There were many irregularities that I noted. The Knights and the Grand Master often held secret meetings at night with a guard posted outside the door. There were men, mostly Knights and Sergeants-at-arms, who would drink to excess. Squires who would sneak out at night or miss prayers or services for spurious reasons. I often witness Templars asleep at prayers. Although it is well known that the Templars have large sums of money, I never saw any location at the commandery where it was stored, and when asked about how it was all accounted for, I was told that if that were my job, I would know."

The Cardinal was silent for a moment, "There are a couple of issues there that would likely result in a letter of reprimand from the Pope, but nothing that would warrant their arrest."

Thomas said, "There is no telling what went on in those secret meetings. That is why I decided to become a member of the Templars so that perhaps I would be allowed into the meetings where I was certain all manner of evil was taking place."

Michael said, "So you took the vows of a Templar Priest so that you…could watch them more closely, and did you witness anything further?"

Thomas replied, "No. I believe they suspected I would not approve of their evil ways and kept me apart from those things."

Michael said, "Later, you encountered this Odo who provided you with stories of the evil that the King was looking for, but as I understand it, these revelations came after the arrests. How and why did Odo seek you out?"

Thomas said, "Just before the arrests, I was sent on a mission with two Knights, a Sergeant-at-arms, and two squires to deliver an object to Rennes la Chateau. Odo was one of the squires. He and I were arrested and sent to separate locations, but when he decided to confess to the evil he had witnessed, he requested to speak to me."

Michael said, "Strange that you were arrested by the same men who sent you to…keep tabs on the Templars. What can you tell me about this, Odo? From what little I have read about this squire, I have been left with the opinion that Odo was either possessed or insane. An opinion that is shared by a couple of men I previously interviewed regarding him."

Thomas wondered who the Cardinal would have interviewed: guards, or perhaps a member of the Inquisition who had been there the first time he had been brought to Odo, who had expressed the same opinion.

Father Thomas said, "Odo was complicated. He had witnessed much evil among the Templars, and I am afraid it had a profound effect on his soul, and concealing the things he witnessed had a lasting impact on his mind. I do not believe he was insane or possessed."

Cardinal Soprano sat looking at Father Thomas for a moment in silence. Father Thomas became clearly uncomfortable with this and had to force himself to remain calm and still.

After several minutes, Cardinal Soprano said, "I'm afraid you do not appreciate this situation. I am not some idiot you can manipulate and lie to."

Father Thomas, suddenly fearful, but feeling he must make some show of indignation, began to stand as if he were going to walk away from this meeting.

Cardinal Soprano said forcefully, "Sit down! I told you we were going to speak freely, and you are going to listen. I DO NOT believe the Templars are guilty of any of the major points the King of France and His motley crew of reprobates accuse them of. I KNOW that Brother Jaye is nothing but a leach on the butt of the King, and he will lie and cheat and kill just to suck a little more blood. And I STRONGLY BELIEVE you are an opportunistic survivor who is a Priest only because you found it an easy way to manipulate others and attain whatever personal goals you have. What I do not know is if any devotion to God and the Truth lies within your soul."

Father Thomas sat silently for a few moments, his mind a blur of thoughts and counterthoughts. He did not know what to do or say.

Chapter 32

The storm battered the ship. Father Loll, who had been at sea several times, was concerned the mast might snap or the sail torn to shreds. Yet, at the same time, the strong winds drove the ship rapidly Eastward, and the rain concealed her. Mary and Father Lull retreated below deck so as not to get in the way of the sailors fighting to keep control in the squall. Derrick, after seeing that Mary and Father Lull were safely below decks, went back on deck to help.

Less than half an hour later, Mary and Father Lull noticed the ship riding more smoothly and could hear that the winds had clearly died down. They both decided to return to the deck to assess the damage caused by the storm. As they stepped into the bright sunshine, they were greatly surprised to see that there was no noticeable damage to the ship, and they had a steady wind moving them north-easterly. Raphael, the first mate, was still at the helm, and he was barking orders to the men to gather some spare canvas from below decks. He told another sailor to go below and get some scrap metal or ceramics they could do without. Then he asked Father Lull, "Good Father, we are going to need to have a funeral. Do you think you could oblige us?"

Father Lull, somewhat flustered, said, "Now? You are going to bury the captain here and now?"

The first mate replied, "Yes, Father, here and now. I don't have the ability to pickle his body to return it to his family, and I don't even know if he has any family. We need to make haste. I don't believe those English ships are still pursuing us, but I don't want to take any chances. The captain lived at sea, and I believe he would want to be laid to rest there also."

Father Lull, noting the tone of anger his questioning of the first mate had caused, simply replied, "I'm sorry, I'm still overcome by the rapidness of the captain's passing. Of course, I am ready."

The first mate then turned to Mary and said, "Young lady, will you go see if you can find the sailmaker? He is sure to be cowering below. Tell him I have need of his needle."

Mary, not liking the disdainful tone in the first mate's voice, simply nodded and went below. She found the sailmaker, Enzo, working with one of the shipwrights, caulking some slats that had begun to leak in the storm. After relaying the message from the first-mate, Enzo gave the shipwright a look of concern and said, "We had best be careful what we say and do. With Raphael in charge, I think the days will grow longer and the meat more salty." The shipwright simply grunted an agreement and returned to his work.

Mary decided to accompany the sailmaker to gather his tools. As they made their way, she asked, "What did you mean by 'the days growing longer and meat more salty'?"

Enzo said, "It's an old saying meaning the work will be hard and the hours will drag on, and the 'meat being more salty' refers to eating old meat stored in salt and indicates that things will become unfair. A Captain at sea is a law unto himself. Captain Timm was a hard but fair man. He made sure we did the work and did it right, but he wasn't a tyrant about it. Now that Raphael is Captain, things are likely to change. Captain Timm was in favor of us continuing with our commitments to the Templars, but Raphael felt that since the Church had moved against the Templars, it was our Catholic duty to abandon them. Most of the crew have served as hired men of the Templars for years and agreed with Captain Timm. Now that Raphael is Captain, who knows what will happen?"

Mary didn't like the sound of that, but there was no time to ask more because they were making their way on deck and to the body of Captain Timm, who they had laid out on a sheet of canvas. Raphael was there with a few other sailors, Derrick, and Father Lull. The man Raphael had sent for scrap metal and ceramic came on deck and said, "This is all I could find, Raphael. It's about four stone. It should be enough."

Without a word, Raphael stepped up to the man and clotted him upside the head with a powerful blow that knocked him to the deck and sent the armload of scrap metal and ceramic tumbling across the deck. As Raphael stood over the kneeling man, he shouted loud enough to be heard from stem to stern, "I am now the captain of this ship, and any one of you that forgets that will find himself receiving a dunking a lot longer and deeper than is comfortable."

The man on the deck said, "I beg your apologies, Captain, Sir." Then he quickly gathered the pieces of metal and ceramic and placed them on the canvas next to Captain Timm's body.

There was a subdued silence after this, and no one seemed to know what to do, and they acted as though they were afraid to move or make a sound. Eventually, Captain Raphael yelled at the sailmaker, "Don't just stand there, sew him in the canvas!"

Enso quickly moved beside Captain Timm's body and got busy sewing. Mary went to the opposite side to help hold the canvas while Enso stitched it closed like a cocoon around Captain Timm. In a few minutes, Enso had the canvas sewn closed, and with a final stitch, he drove the needle through Captain Timm's nose. This shocked Mary, and she wondered if Enso had some grudge against the dead Captain, but didn't feel it was the time or place to ask.

As soon as the final stitch was made, Captain Raphael looked at Father Lull and said, "Father."

Father Lull led the group in an Our Father prayer, then said, "Lord God, by the power of your Word, you stilled the chaos of the primeval seas, you made the raging waters of the Flood subside, and calmed the storm on the sea of Galilee. As we commit the earthly remains
of our brother Captain Timm to the deep, grant him peace and tranquility until that day when he and all who believe in You will be raised to the glory of new life promised in the waters of baptism. We ask this through Christ, our Lord. In the name of the Father, the Son, and the Holy Spirit. Amen"

The body, shrouded in the canvas coffin, was lifted to the shoulders of six of the sailors, who carried it to the side of the ship and dropped it over. It took a moment for the trapped air in the canvas to escape, but soon it drifted below the seas, dragged down by the weight of the metal and ceramic.

Captain Raphael then shouted, "Get that sail up. We have a long voyage ahead of us."

Later that night, when Mary, Father Lull, and Derrick were below deck and reasonably alone, Mary asked what the other two thought of the new Captain. Father Lull said, "It's hard to tell yet. He had to assume command in an instant, and that often requires a harsh hand to establish his authority and keep the men on track. Captain Timm was popular with the men, and that often makes it difficult for the succeeding captain to follow. What has me concerned is that I have heard a few of the men talking, and I'm not sure, but I don't believe the captain is still taking us and this shipment to meet with the other Ships. I will talk to him about it in the morning, but I feel that with all that transpired today, I shouldn't bring it up yet."

Mary looked at Derrick, waiting for his response. Realizing he had to say something, Derrick finally said, "We'll see."

Mary, clearly not happy with these assessments of the new Captain, said, "I'm not going to just sit and see what happens. I am tired of feeling like I have no choices either because I'm a woman or because I'm poor and of no consequence." Having said that, she stormed off to find Captain Raphael.

The captain was also below deck. He was reviewing charts and speaking with the new First Mate. When Mary found them, she asked the captain, "Captain, I beg your pardon, but I heard that we are no longer heading to Germany. Where are you taking the possessions of the Templars you have in your hold?"

Captain Raphael slowly turned to face Mary and replied, "I am the captain of this vessel, and I will keep my own counsel. I do not have a need to listen to your opinions, nor do I have any reason to seek your approval. If I decide to tell you where I am taking the vessel under my command, I will inform you; otherwise, you are free to disembark at any time you see fit." Then he returned his attention to the charts

Mary waited a moment, feeling the heat rise in her face, but realizing there was nothing she could do at this time that would not open her up to further mockery, she turned to make her way back to Father Lull and Derrick. As she left, the captain looked at his First Mate and said, "That is precisely the reason women should not be allowed on ships. For some reason, the sea air makes them think they have a justification for opening their mouth and saying whatever stupid thing pops into their simple mind." The First Mate dutifully laughed.

Chapter 33

Louis was off with a group of Scots practicing with sword, shield, and halberd. There were about twenty in the group, but only six were warriors; the others were a mix of children and women. They were about a mile from the town in a semi-isolated spot where they often practiced. The children ran off to play hide and seek in the nearby woods, and women mostly made fun of those who practiced at war. It was a bright sunny day, one of the few since Louis had arrived. Practicing with the Scotts was always very different from practicing with William or any of the training he received as Templar squire. Templar training was regimented and progressed from one thing to the next. Warming up with slow, rudimentary sword movements, then half-speed drills, followed by full-speed drills until your arms and legs were about to fall off, a brief water break, and then back at it before your muscles could cool down. The practice continued with either foot or horse combat, which consisted of attacking one another until the Knight or Sergeant-at-Arms in charge called for them to quit. Then the squires would cool down by cleaning and repairing arms and armor, and caring for the horses, while the Knights and Sergeants-at-Arms continued to practice more complex drills.

The Scotts, on the other hand, didn't bother with any preliminaries. They squared off in pairs or groups and went about attacking one another until they were mostly exhausted, lying on the ground. There were no rules to the practice; you might find yourself fighting one-on-one with someone, and one or two others might attack you from behind, or one of the men who had had enough and was sitting on the ground might find a rock and throw it at your head. Louis thought it too haphazard to be of much benefit at first, but he soon discovered he was learning to keep more aware of his surroundings and watch more for openings in defenses he had never noticed before. Additionally, it was more enjoyable. There was a certain amount of lighthearted juvenile fun in these practices that was clearly absent from the standardized methods the Templars used.

After two rounds of this melee practice, the warriors were all sitting and laughing and enjoying the sun when one of the children came running out of the woods yelling, "There are men in the woods. They killed Calum." The girl was only about twenty feet from the tree line when the group of Scots saw an arrow flying out of the woods. The girl fell on her face, an arrow protruding from her back.

Louis and the six Scottish warriors were instantly on their feet, grabbing swords and shields and moving quickly toward the fallen girl with several of the women following. As they reached the girl, a few more arrows came out of the darkness of the trees, so the men made a protective arch of shields between the woods and the girl. The warriors all knelt to allow the shields to cover as much of the area as possible. One of the women with them grabbed the arrow with one hand, just above where it had entered the girl's back, then, with her other hand, she snapped the rest of the arrow off and tossed it aside. Then the woman lifted the girl and said to Finley, the oldest and most experienced of the fighters, "I'm ready." They all rose to a crouch and backed away from the woods at a steady but controlled pace.

Louis was amazed at how the group worked together without a word being spoken to them and was again impressed by these people. A few minutes ago, they were all joking and seemed to have no cares, and a moment later, they came together in complete seriousness and acted as a fluid unit, including the women. Several of the women had instantly run off toward the town to get help, while three had stayed to help retrieve the injured girl. Louis knew without asking that they would not enter the woods to get the other children. They were either already dead, had fled, or were hiding. As they got about 100 yards from the trees, a group of about twenty men stepped out of the woods.

Finley said with a growl in his voice, "Those are Comyn's men. What are those bastards doing here?"

Finley yelled to the three women carrying the child, "Keep going! Run as fast as ya can."

The six warriors and Louis all stopped in a line, back near where they had been practicing. Since the archer had stopped shooting, they all stood up straight with their shields at their side. The Comyn men who had emerged from the woods broke into a run, charging the seven. The men who ran at them were prepared for battle, and Louis was sure their weapons held keen edges. While Louis and his six companions had practice weapons. They were real swords and halberds, but as practice weapons, their edges were blunted. They could still kill, but it would take hard, crushing blows or powerful thrusts.

The seven men interlocked their shields, and Finley said, "Stay together, lads. We fight as one man today. This is proving to be an interesting day, and as the old croon says, 'May ya be cursed to live in interesting times.'"

At that moment, the other group of warriors crashed into them. For Louis, it all turned into a clash of shields and blades. He and the six warriors he fought with tried to keep their shields together, but with so many men attacking them, they could not remain in a line, and they were forced to form a small, rough circle as the other men took station around them. Before they were able to close the circle, Finley was struck a savage blow to his face and fell to the ground.

Louis could not pay much attention to what happened after that. Blow after blow fell on his shield, and at least one of the attackers had a pike that had repeatedly tried to reach him by attacking over the top of his shield. The pikeman soon stopped its' annoying attacks. Louis didn't know if it was because the man was killed or just moved on to a different person to pester. Although Louis received no serious injuries, he was grazed by many blows to areas where his armor was weak or open. He also had no idea if he struck any killing blows. He knew he struck many of the attackers with great force, but the whole situation was constantly in motion. He might glimpse a face over the edge of a shield and make a thrust or swing an overhand blow that struck something or someone, but then there would appear another shield and another face. He was unaware of the passage of time; he lost any sense of where his companions were, and he had no idea how many men were left to either side. Everything deteriorated to a series of swings, blocks, thrusts, parries, slams, holds, punches, steps back, pivots to the right, faints, swings back around, and ducks. There was no thought; it was just muscle memory and training.

At some point, all the pressure abruptly ceased. Louis's attackers had backed away, and he got his first clear picture of the situation around him. Men lay bleeding and dying or already dead all around him. He saw most of the men whom he had been training with just a short time ago lying on the bloody grass. He looked at the men who still surrounded him but had backed away just out of sword range. Louis was still crouched in a defensive stance behind his shield, and he could tell one of the men was speaking to him, but he couldn't hear what he said due to the ringing in his ears caused by adrenaline and the numerous sword strikes to his helmet. As his heart rate and breathing came under control, he finally began to make out what the man was saying.

"...no reason for you to die. Your companions are all dead. You still face twelve of us who are uninjured. You look on the verge of collapsing. You fought well, but this is at an end; drop your sword."

Louis stood up straighter and looked around himself with clearer comprehension now as the fog, or whatever it was that took over once the fight started, faded. He started to speak, but his throat was so dry he couldn't make a sound; he tried to swallow, but his mouth was like a desert. He tried to cough, but that only brought the pounding in his ears back.

The man who had spoken before said, "We don't need a speech. Just drop your sword, you killed several of my men. I have seen a few men fight with your skill, but I won't give you a chance to kill another. By yourself, we can keep our distance and shoot you with an arrow or attack you with a pike."

Louis, the pounding in his head growing louder, lowered back into a fighting stance, his shield out front, his eyes peering over the top, and his sword raised over his head, the blade parallel to the ground. These men had killed his friends; he would never surrender to them.

The man facing him said, "This is foolish, but if you want to die, so be it." Then he looked to his left and said, "Karl, try not to miss and hit any of us with a stray arrow." But as he finished saying this, Louis noticed that the men facing him all turned to look behind them. It was then that Louis realized the pounding was not in his head.

Over the crest of the hill came four men on horseback, led by William and Cinead. As the soldiers, who had been about to finish off Louis, focused their attention on this new threat. Louis charged forward and plunged his dull practice sword through the exposed neck of the man who had told him to surrender. Before any of his men could react, the four riders were upon them.

Chapter 34

The room Henry and his nine companions waited in was not very large, and they occupied almost the entire space. The Priest had said nothing more as he led them there and only told them to wait quietly before he left. There were no windows in the room, only the door they had entered from the outside and another on the far wall through which the priests had exited. When they had checked the doors after the priest had departed, they were not surprised to find them locked. That had been several minutes ago, and they were all growing antsy except for Garrard de La Languedoc, who leaned calmly against a wall.

Henry made his way to Garrard and said just above a whisper, "How can you be so calm? We could have been led here as part of a trap. We cannot effectively defend ourselves crammed in a locked room."

Garrard said calmly, "We knew when we left on this mission, it would likely not end well. We all agreed it was worth it and that we had to do something. And now, with this little twist, we have a better chance than I believed possible. As far as I can see, it doesn't really matter if they decide to kill us here. If we'd have continued back to the Hospitaller commandery, we'd surely be arrested and sent to the King. If we decided to hide in the city and attempt to sneak out through the gates, there's a good chance we'd be caught and sent to the King."

Henry was about to respond when the door that the priest had left by reopened. A man in cardinal robes entered the crowded room. Over the Cardinal's shoulder, Henry could see the priest who led them here.

The Cardinal said, "You gentlemen have created quite a stir. I am Cardinal David. I was sent here by the Holy Father to see if I could gather a few of the Knights of the Order who are locked in the dungeons by the King of this fair land, but King Philip has not seen fit to see me."

Henry asked, "Why does the Pope want the Templars to be held by the King?"

The Cardinal replied, "Generally, to rescue them from the clutches of this Monarch who seems to believe his Throne holds more power than the seat of Saint Peter. The specifics of exactly what will happen to the Templars I have been attempting to gain access to had not been worked out at the time I departed Avignon."

Henry then asked, "And what do you want with us?"

The Cardinal said, "I wish to help you out of the city and have you travel back with me to Avignon to see the Pope and from there get you out of France to a location where you can continue your devotion to God and the Church."

Sir Garrard asked, "It appears to us that the Holy Father may not be entirely on our side in this matter. Why should we believe we would be any safer in Avignon than we would be in the dungeons of King Philip?"

Cardinal David said, with a hint of anger in his tone, "You have no idea how the Holy Father feels or what He wishes in this matter. His hands have been restricted due to the actions and accusations of the King of France, and this has not been aided by the confessions of your members, especially within your leadership. The Pope is doing all He can to protect the members of His flock from the well-executed and flagrant attack by the King and his sycophants."

Henry said, "It doesn't appear much has been done from our perspective."

The Cardinal said, now with much more than a hint of anger, "Keeping all this secret is due to necessity. What is happening and what has already been done to protect as many of you as possible must be kept confidential for the time being. Trust me, the things that are done in darkness will soon be brought to light. This includes not only the evil actions of King Philip but also the glorious actions of the Holy Father. Your little stunt today will make things more difficult for us to extract more Templars from the King. Although there was little chance he would release any Templars to me anyway."

Calmed down, the Cardinal continued, "As for the ten of you. If you accept my offer to take you to Avignon, I will have you remove your armor and don the robes of monks and hide here for a few days until we depart. I will leave you alone to discuss what you will choose to do, but your decision will need to be unanimous and made quickly."

After the Cardinal and the priest left, Henry said, "Well, boys, what do you say? Do we trust the Cardinal who comes out of nowhere and says he's been sent here by the Pope to rescue us Templars? Or do we return to the Hospitaller's commandery, where we are sure to be handed over to the King, who has previously imprisoned and tortured us? Or do we try to make a run for it on our own?"

The deliberation did not take long. Brother Jamison, the mason, was the only one who wasn't sure trusting the Cardinal was the best choice, but in the end, he agreed that the other options were probably worse. By the time the Cardinal returned, all the Templars had removed their armor. The Cardinal seemed pleased by the decision and soon had brown monk robes, along with bread and wine, brought in for them.

Chapter 35

Cardinal Soprano was waiting for Father Thomas to respond. Thomas finally looked Cardinal Soprano in the eyes and said, "Your Eminence, to be completely honest…"

Cardinal Soprano held up a hand for Father Thomas to stop and signed loudly, "Let me stop you before you lie to me again. In my many years of listening to confessions, I have found one thing to be true as an absolute certainty: anytime someone starts with a statement promising that they are about to tell me the truth, they are going to lie. Let me clarify my intentions and lay them before you, and then you can decide what you wish to do and say.

"I am not with the inquisition, as you well know, I do not agree with their methods, and although they are sanctioned by the Holy Church, I question their effectiveness and reason for being. I am not here to get you to confess anything that is not true. I wish to know two things: I want to know the truth about the evidence you have provided, particularly the statements you claim Odo the squire made. Secondly, I want to redeem your soul for God. I believe that if you ever took your vows to God and the Church seriously, you have long since cast them adrift in favor of seeking personal goals of this world. I can tell you are an intelligent man; I just can't tell if there is any integrity, charity, and piety to balance that intelligence."

Father Thomas, who stared intently at Cardinal Soprano's face the entire time, started to speak, but, again, Cardinal Soprano raised his hand in a gesture indicating Father Thomas should remain silent.

Cardinal Soprano continued, "Let me finish. I make no threats other than this: if you choose to continue lying, I will ensure that you are defrocked, not as a punishment, but because if your vows were and are false, then you are not a true representative of the Holy Roman Church. If you are a true son of The Church and a faithful servant of God, then I will use my considerable influence to find a place within the Church where you can be an effective minister of God's love and grace."

Father Thomas found himself fearful of this man. Not in the same way he was afraid of Brother Jaye or the Inquisition. The fear was not merely a visceral, animal-like fear; it was deeper and more profound. He knew he could always lie to the Inquisition, tell them whatever they wanted to hear, and at least have a chance, but here, with this man, he did not know how to respond. He thought there was still a chance he could lie, but he'd have to be careful that all his lies were made up of only truths. He'd done this before, but usually, it was in a setting where he was dealing with legal matters and others who had been trained in the law. In that setting, they were all playing the same game, and the rules were clear. If you could establish a "truth" that allowed you to use the system to get what they wanted, then even if it wasn't completely fair to some, they could claim it was justice. Here and now, Thomas could see that the situation with Cardinal Soprano was entirely different. He did not want to know truths; he wanted THE TRUTH. Thomas was not sure he knew what THE TRUTH was. Thomas knew that everything we perceive as truth is clouded by our own prejudices, preconceived ideas, previous experiences, and personal goals. How can he lay all those things aside and look at the core of an issue and see the truth? Furthermore, did he really want to? Life was hard enough; did he truly want to start examining issues without first considering what he personally had to gain or lose from the outcome?

Father Thomas finally decided his best bet was to stall and hope things would change once again. Why should he play by Cardinal Soprano's rules? So, he said in a sincere tone, "You have given me a great deal to consider, Your Eminence. I would like to contemplate the matter and spend some time in prayer."

Cardinal Soprano said, "No. There is nothing to pray about; God assuredly wants you to speak the truth. And although I'm sure the truth might be hard for you to find at first, buried under the mounds of manure, you have hidden it beneath, but I'm sure if you try, you will be able to get a hand on it and begin the task of drawing it out. As you expose it to the light, you will find the truth becomes easier for you to recognize."

Father Thomas felt like an animal must when it was trapped in a snare. He wanted to get away, to run and hide, but apparently, that was not going to happen. Finally, he said, "Ok, Cardinal Soprano, what exactly do you want to know?"

Cardinal Soprano, who had been leaning forward in his chair, leaned back and said, "Let us start with what Guillaume de Norgaret charged you to learn about the Templars and what you actually witnessed."

Father Thomas took a breath and said, "Guillaume de Norgaret had me brought to his offices and told me that I was to find whatever incriminating evidence I could regarding the Templars. He told me they were no better than Jews with their loan practices and that they needed to be brought to justice for their multitude of sins. He said that if I could provide clear evidence against them, I would be handsomely rewarded. After the first few weeks, I reported back that there were a few drunkards among the Order and that they held secret meetings, but other than that, I didn't see anything.

"Guillaume de Nogaret said that he knew for a fact that there was evil and corruption among the Knights and that I was to do whatever it took to discover evidence of that fact. He also added that if I did not find what he knew was going on with the Templar Order, he could only assume that I had been tempted into complicity with them. Upon returning to the Paris Commandery, I told them of my desire to join the Order as a Priest in the hopes that I would then discover the evidence Guillaume de Norgaret desired. I was soon to find out that my status as a Templar Priest made no real difference. Only Knights and Sergeants were allowed into the meetings.

"Then, after the arrests, there was confusion about my connection with the Order until I was brought to help with Odo, whom I knew before the arrests. At first, I thought that Odo was the answer the Crown was looking for, but as time went on, I began to see that Odo had suffered some type of event while being held by the King's men that did something to his memory and his reasoning ability. I feared that if I revealed this to Brother Jaye, I would be accused of sympathizing with the Templars, whom the King and the

Inquisition now fully believed had committed some truly evil atrocities.

"Shortly before Odo's death, he seemed to come back to himself and told me that he didn't know why he was saying all the terrible things about the Templars. He didn't feel like it was himself saying them, but someone else, and he was only an observer. I don't think that, at that point, he believed what he had previously told me was true. I do not believe he was possessed, but I could not say for sure."

Cardinal Soprano then replied, "And what of yourself, Father Thomas?"

Father Thomas was not certain what he meant. "What do you mean? Are you asking if I am possessed?"

Cardinal Soprano laughed, "No, not at all. I'm asking about your soul. Are you truly a son of the True Faith and committed to God and your fellow man? Or are you just another member of the clergy out selling indulgences and whatever else you can to make yourself more comfortable?"

Father Thomas thought for a moment, then said, "I am not sure. Although I decided to become a priest because it was a path that I thought would keep me from starvation I did learn to love the knowledge it allowed me to learn and there was a time when I felt a devotion to God, but I'm not sure I've ever truly felt anything like love or compassion for my fellow man. I thought I could serve God with my mind, if not my heart."

Cardinal Soprano said, "I think Father Thomas, that perhaps you can be of use to God and the Holy Father after all. Now might be a good time for prayer, reflection, and confession. If you are so inclined, there are several chapels here and several Priests who would hear your confession. I have work I must attend to now. We will talk again tomorrow."

Chapter 36

Mary was still fuming below decks the next morning when Derrick went above to help the other sailors. She held a wooden mallet in one hand and was absently tapping the caulking further into the seams between the planks of the ship. Just after sunup, Father Lull had asked Captain Raphael about where the ship was heading and if he still intended to meet up with the other Templar ships as planned. The captain had also refused to explain his intentions to the priest. Mary, Derrick, and Father Lull were certain the captain had no intention of taking this ship to the rendezvous point. The question was, where were they headed now?

Father Lull sat beside her and said, "Things are different at sea than on land. A Captain is in charge and does not need to listen to any of the members of his crew. A good Captain knows when to listen and when to ignore the crew's counsel. Yet regardless of whether he listens to others or not, every decision is his own, and he alone is responsible for everything that happens."

Mary, not caring to hear more of the difficult situation Captain Raphael had found himself in, said, "Did you know that when Enso was sewing Captain Timm in the canvas, he forcefully drove the needle through the captain's nose?! Do these men harbor some resentment toward Captain Timm? I just don't understand how things could have changed so drastically and so quickly."

Father Lull said, "Driving the needle through the captain's nose is normal. It is one last test to make sure the man is dead before we commit his body to the deep. If the man were only unconscious, we would expect some movement from this. As far as the change in the attitude of the crew and the heading of the ship, well..."

Just then, they both heard what sounded like a fight up on deck. Soon after, one of the deckhands stuck his head through a hatch and said to them, "You may want to get up on deck. The captain is going to dunk your friend."

Mary had heard the term "dunking" being mentioned a few times while aboard ship, but had no idea what it really meant. As they quickly made their way up on deck, she asked Father Lull, "What is 'dunking'?"

Father Lull said, "Well, it is a punishment of sorts used on ships. The severity of it varies significantly. At times, dunking is something done almost for fun. Once, when I was aboard another ship, I was dunked. Essentially, they attach a shortboard to a line that is running up the yardarm, creating a type of seat that can be swung out over the water and then raised and lowered. The individual being dunked sits on the board, tied in, and is swung out over the water; some of the line is played out, and the person is dunked into the sea. Now, if the individual is being dunked more for fun than punishment, they are basically dunked and completely soaked once or twice, and then brought back on deck. That's what happened to me, and I found it very enjoyable and invigorating. But if it is used as a real punishment, the individual is left in the water and may be dunked a few feet below the surface. Some get left down long enough that they nearly drown, and many times, the man can be repeatedly dunked. Once I witnessed a man dunked so long and deeply several times that I was surprised he survived."

Just then, the two stepped through the hatch onto the deck. The first thing Mary noticed was Derrick, who appeared unconscious, being tied to the seat that Father Lull had just described. Captain Raphael was standing by the side rail, looking out to sea, just next to Derrick, with his hands clasped behind his back, looking as though nothing was going on. Lying on the deck was the still-dripping body of the cabin boy. Mary ran toward Derrick and was stopped just short by one of the sailors, who grabbed her by the shoulders and stopped her. He spoke to her in a voice only she could hear and said, "Stop, young Miss, you can't stop this, and trying to will only make it worse."

Before Mary could even think of what to say, Father Lull spoke up, "Captain Raphael, may I ask what is going on?"

For a moment, Mary thought the captain might not respond, but then he slowly turned and said in a calm voice, "This man attempted to interfere with my command of this vessel and her crew, and as a result, he shall be punished so that he may learn discipline."

Father Lull went to the cabin boy and, upon inspecting him, said, "Captain, this boy is dead."

The captain ignored the Priest and said, "Hoist the seat and swing it out over the water."

"Aye aye, Captain." Yelled one of the men as they pulled on the line, raising the seat Derrick was now firmly tied to.

As Derrick was swung out over the water, Mary saw that he was reviving. As the seat was suspended above the water about ten feet off the side of the ship, the captain commanded, "Play out the line."

The sailors began to let the line out, and Derrick hit the water just as he began to look around, still clearly dazed and unsure what was happening. The sailors continued to let out line, and for a moment, Derrick skipped on the water before he disappeared below the waves. Mary, now released by the sailor who had held her, ran to the side rail and stared at the rope where it entered the cold black water. After what seemed a long time, she looked back at the captain, who had resumed his unconcerned manner, looking loftily off into the distant sea, and screamed, "Pull him out! You're going to kill him!"

The captain looked as though he hadn't heard. After several more seconds, Father Lull said, "Captain?"

Captain Raphael looked toward the men holding the line and waved his hand, indicating they should haul in the line. As they pulled as rapidly as they could, Derrick broke the surface, and Mary noticed he didn't appear to be breathing. As she was about to cry out, he coughed out water and began sputtering for air. Just as his eyes fluttered open and he was about to take a breath without coughing, Captain Raphael commanded the men holding the line, "Play out the line. Dunk him again." The men hesitated just a moment, and the captain rounded on them, screaming in a frantic state, "That was an ORDER! Lower him, NOW!" The men played out the line, and Derrick once more vanished beneath the surface of the water.

Mary was filled with a sudden, blinding rage. This Captain was a tyrant, and he had already killed the poor cabin boy and was trying to kill Derrick. She couldn't just stand by and watch. She had lived a life of servitude, having to grovel for mere survival, and still, men tried to take what little she called her own from her. The belief grew from the time she was a young child; she was taught not to trust her feelings that told her to act against someone in authority over her, no matter what they said or did. The training only intensified as she grew older; she was made to feel that she was ignorant and that her thoughts and feelings did not matter. It was not only her, but also all the women she knew. It had been ground into them so deeply that they believed that as a gender, they were inferior and only useful as servants, whores, or mothers. Even when she had accidentally hit the man who tried to rape her with her head and then run away, she had felt guilty, as if her not allowing him to have his way with her meant there was something wrong with her. After meeting Derrick and later Father Lull, she began to realize that her thoughts and feelings mattered. That she had the right to express her thoughts and to have her ideas honestly considered. That she could and should act on what she knew was right.

She had to do something! She knew appealing to the captain would do nothing except perhaps make things worse. She frantically looked around for someone or something to help. None of the sailors would make eye contact with her; they all feared the captain too much. Father Lull was a few feet away, speaking to the captain, pleading with him to haul in the line. The captain stood between Father Lull and herself. He was turned sideways and again ignored everything on the ship, acting as though he could hear nothing. It was then that Mary realized she was still holding the wooden mallet she had been using when the sailor came below deck to get her and Father Lull. Before anyone could react, and even before she truly considered what she was doing, she took two quick steps toward the captain, raising the mallet as she moved and brought it down, using all the anger and frustration that had built up inside her to strike Captain Raphael soundly on the back of his skull. The captain crumpled to the deck unconscious. Mary turned to the men holding the line and yelled at them, "Haul in the line, now!"

This time, the men did not hesitate at all and quickly pulled together, bringing in the line and raising Derrick out of the water. By the time they had brought him up and swung the seat, he was tied to back over the deck, Mary could see he was alive.

Father Lull looked at Mary and then at the captain's unmoving form on the deck. Mary went to the new first mate, whose name she didn't know, and handed him the mallet. Then she went to Derrick, who was lying on the deck, trying to push himself to his feet.

The first mate looked around the deck for a moment; most of the sailors were looking at him. The first mate moved to where the captain lay and asked Father Lull, "Father, would you be so good as to check the captain and see if he is still among the living?"

Father Lull knelt beside the captain and checked his skull where Mary had struck him; the area was matted with blood, but it was not flowing. Outwardly, it appeared to be a superficial wound. The captain was breathing but unresponsive. Father Lull said, "The Captain is alive, only unconscious."

The first mate said in an even, clear tone, "That is unfortunate. Nothing we can do about it now. Then he shouted to the men on deck, "You four, take the captain below and secure him hand and foot until we can decide what to do with him, and two of you remain there with him. The rest of you clean this mess up and get young Peter's body ready for burial."

Then, in a lower tone, he said to Father Lull, "As soon as Derrick can stand, you three are to meet me on the aft fighting castle." And then he walked to the back of the ship.

Chapter 37

The fight was over in an instant once William, Cinead, and the others arrived. The first four riders were followed by five more, and then several men on foot came in just in time to take the surrender of the four enemy survivors that remained standing. Louis was on his knees trying to catch his breath by then. As it turned out, three of the six men Louis had been practicing with before the attack took place were still alive, and they're injuries were being tended to.

The four prisoners knelt on the ground while Cinead walked in front of them. He reached down and grabbed one by the front of his gambeson and held a knife to his throat. He asked the man, "I see you are of Comyn's clan. What are you doing here?"

The man spat in Cinead's face, which resulted in a flash of blood as Cinead opened the man's throat from ear to ear. Cinead let the lifeless corpse drop, then he said to the other three prisoners, "That was a brave and honorable act from your friend, but he is now dead, and his bravery will soon be forgotten. Let us see how many more brave, honorable, and soon-to-be-forgotten men we have here today." Cinead grabbed a second man and looked him in the eyes while he held the blood-covered knife up for him to see and said, "You know, lad, I don't think I'll be needing this. Where should I put it? I cannot put it back in the scabbard, all covered in blood, that nearly ruins the leather, and the blade ends up all rusty. I can't just toss it aside; it's a fine knife. Do you think you can hold onto it for me?" Cinead flipped the knife down, which buried itself all the way to the hilt in the man's foot. The man yelled in pain but soon regained control.

Cinead said, "There's a good lad. Now, just to be clear, I won't be killing any of ya outright like I did your poor forgotten friend there. No, I need answers, and I need them now. You see that man there? The one that held off the lot of you so the rest of us could arrive. That man is a Knight Templar, and over there on that horse sits another Templar, and not too far over those hills, I've got a whole passel of Knights Templar. I suppose you've heard tell of the tortures the Inquisition put these men through. They've been telling me all sorts of stories; some I can't believe a man can survive, and I'd like to see for myself just how much a man can take and remain alive. So, I'm kind of hoping you will not answer too quickly."

Before Cinead could say more, one of the two men left kneeling said, "It makes no difference now anyway. We were sent to assess the area, confirm Robert the Bruce's presence, identify your defenses, and report back. We have already determined that your numbers were too great to attack at this time. The only good news we discovered is that Robert the Bruce is still sick, and maybe he won't recover. If he dies, there'd be no more call for fighting between us Scots, and I can get back to killing Englishmen. We were on our way back when one of our men ran headlong into some of your children playing in the woods. He killed the boy out of instinct, and I am sorry for the lad's mother. The order to shoot the girl with the bow came from our leader, Niall, who was a bloody coward, and I'm personally glad yon Templar sent him off to Hell."

Cinead reached down and yanked the knife out of the man's foot and said to the women who were tending the wounded, "Take care of this lad's injury."

Later that afternoon, after Louis had eaten and bathed in a cold spring, he was approached by William and Cinead. Cinead said, "From all accounts, you fought well out there. Even the survivors of those who attacked you admitted to being impressed by your skill. Our lads that survived said if it wasn't for you, they would all have been slaughtered before help could arrive."

Louis, embarrassed, said, "I don't know how anyone can make a statement like that. It was all confusion. I can't clearly recall any details of what took place."

William said, "It's often that way in the heat of battle, but Cinead is not exaggerating, for once. All the men spoke of your ferocity, skill, and bravery in the battle."

Cinead asked William, "Why is this man still a squire? I know you Templars think your skill at arms is akin to Michael the Archangel, but surely this lad meets even your standards. And by-God, he's old enough. If he were one of us, he'd have been knighted and have several men to command, a wife, and a couple of children by now."

William said, "Discipline was always lacking when we discussed knighting him in counsel. We Templars do not knight individuals ourselves. We are each knighted by a monarch or some other Lord outside of our Order. And of late, we've been avoiding Kings and the like."

Cinead slapped Louis on the back, which sent a wave of pain through his bruised and battered body, and said with a laugh, "Well, lad, let's at least get you something to eat and drink, and perhaps you can sneak away from the prudish Templars long enough to find some comfort in a woman's breast. After today, I'd say you deserve it, but stay away from my daughters, or I'll remove your head and toss it in the sea, so in Heaven, you'll either be headless or bodiless, depending on where the Priests decide your soul resides. Although perhaps we should get you married, I had a couple of children by the time I was your age. I noticed your eye on Isla the other night; she's a fair lass and single. I'll speak to her father for you."

Before Louis could respond, Cinead had walked away.

Chapter 38

Henry, having never been a patient man, was getting very frustrated by all the waiting. It was more than two weeks before their group left Paris. As they left the city, the Cardinal rode in a wagon, and a few of the priests rode horses, but most of them, including all the Templars, walked. There was no confrontation as they left Paris; the procession simply walked out through one of the city gates. It took nearly three weeks to reach Avignon at the leisurely pace the Cardinal insisted upon.

Once they arrived, the Templars were all brought into the building reserved for the Cardinals, where they were instructed to continue to behave as brother monks and work as servants for the Cardinals and priests. They were not to interact with one another except in a manner as would be normally expected, and they were not to reveal their identity to anyone except the Cardinals, who had all already been informed of their identity.

On the second day after arriving in Avignon, Henry nearly destroyed the veil of secrecy of who they were. As he was walking across the common yard carrying a load of firewood, he saw a priest he recognized walking with a Cardinal. Before Henry realized what he was doing, he had dropped the firewood except for one club-sized piece and sprang across the yard straight at Father Thomas. Henry most likely would have killed Father Thomas if not for the Cardinal, who was clearly stronger than his robes made him look, and must have had some instruction in fighting. As Henry reached the pair, he ignored the Cardinal, rage making him focus on Father Thomas. Just as he was about to swing the improvised club, the Cardinal caught his arm in a powerful grip and, with his other hand, he took the club from Henry, then, using Henry's own momentum, the Cardinal pitched Henry to the ground before he could do any harm to Father Thomas.

Sir Henry, Knight of the Temple, had almost always been the best fighter on any practice field he had been on since he was a young boy. Now he found himself flat on his back, trying to catch the breath that had been knocked out of him, which was not being made any easier by the foot of the Cardinal that had rested on his chest. Henry looked up at the Cardinal and saw that he held a piece of firewood Henry had been going to use to beat Father Thomas with and had it pointed at Henry's nose.

Cardinal Soprano said in an unnervingly calm voice, "Young brother, I am not certain why you came running at us brandishing a stick with murder in your eyes, although I can guess." As he gave a sidelong glance at Father Thomas, he continued, "I promise you this: if you attempt to rise from the ground with anger in your heart, I will knock you silly with this piece of wood. Although I'm sure I will be justified in my righteous anger, I also know it will require some time in prayer and an Act of Contrition on my part, and my schedule is quite full for the next few days. Before you respond, I want you to understand that I am a firm believer in the Holy Scriptures and am particularly fond of the verse that tells us 'Whatever you find to do with your hands do with all you might...'"

Henry, still shaking with anger, forced himself to calm down. Before he spoke, he took a deep breath and calmed his racing heart, "Your Eminence, I'm not sure you know the true nature of the man beside you. I promise you, I will not harm him at this time if you hear me out regarding Father Thomas."

Cardinal Soprano said, "I don't believe we can know the true nature of any man, possibly not even ourselves. I will listen to you, and we will have this conversation in private shortly, but right now, you should rise before this altercation draws any more attention."

The Cardinal then reached down his free hand and helped Henry up, handed him the stick of firewood, and said, "You had better complete your duties and then meet Father Thomas and me in the library, which is through the doors just ahead of us. I will expect you shortly. If you have more tasks, let the cooks know that I require your assistance. I am Cardinal Soprano."

In less than five minutes, Henry walked through the door to the library where Father Thomas and Cardinal Soprano waited. At the sight of Father Thomas, Henry felt the anger rise in him again. Father Thomas had cost him his freedom and caused him to be tortured for crimes he hadn't committed. Because of the betrayal of

Father Thomas, he had no idea what became of his squire, Odo, and that girl, Mary, who had been traveling with them. Henry stopped and forced himself to calm down before he continued to where the other two waited.

As Henry approached, Cardinal Soprano said, "Sir Henry de Creon, Father Thomas has informed me of who you are and has just now conveyed to me why you are so angry with him."

Henry said more forcefully than he intended, "I would be surprised if he didn't leave a few things out of the explanation."

Cardinal Soprano replied, "Be that as it may, the father would like to make his apologies."

Father Thomas said, "I am sorry for my betrayal of you and Odo. I was operating under some assumptions that over the last few weeks, Cardinal Soprano has helped me to understand were false. Although I don't expect you to believe me, everything I did was done because I thought it was the right thing to do. I believed the Templars were corrupt and seeking to do great harm to the Holy Roman Church. I was wrong and I am sorry. It may help if you know that I, too, suffered and was treated falsely. Additionally, I was reacquainted with Odo; he came to trust me, and we aided one another in that dark time."

Henry looked at Thomas, then at Cardinal Soprano, and sputtered, "Are you expecting me to believe anything this creature says? If he told me it was raining, I would go outside to check. He has done nothing but attempt to achieve his own desires, no matter the cost to those around him. I can hardly stand here without throttling him, much less forgive him. I don't know what you wish of me."

Cardinal Soprano said, "I hope in time you will forgive Father Thomas, as it appears he will play a role in what the Holy Father has planned for you and the group of Templars you arrived with. At this time, I just wanted you to hear him out, and I would have you consider that the Scripture teaches that God has made many types of vessels, some for honor and some for destruction, and it is not our job to judge God on how He made us or others. It is also not for us to judge how God chooses to use His vessels. He is God, and it is His choice."

Henry looked at Father Thomas, who kept his head bowed, looking at the floor. He wanted to exact his revenge on him, but at least for now, he would control himself. He sighed loudly and said, "Ok, I will not attempt to harm the…good…Father, but I will not trust him. I do have some questions I'd like answered. You mentioned that the Holy Father has plans for me and the others who came with me. What are those plans? And where is Odo?"

Chapter 39

Mary, Derrick, Father Lull, and the First Mate stood on the raised platform at the back of the ship. The First Mate looked at Derrick and said, "Are you ok?"

Derrick replied by nodding his head in the affirmative. Although if he were honest, he would like to go lie down out of the sun somewhere. His ears made everything muffled, and his head hurt from when Captain Raphael had bashed him on the back of the head.

The First Mate then said, "My name is Jacques, and I intend to take command of the ship even if Captain Raphael recovers. After what he did to young Peter, I don't think the crew would balk at my taking charge."

Father Lull asked, "What happened with Peter, and why was Derrick being dunked?"

They all knew Derrick was not going to respond, so Jacques said, "Captain Raphael gave Peter an order, and the lad in his haste replied, 'Yes, Sir, Captain Timm.' The captain flew into a rage and ordered the men to rig for dunking. The entire time the men were preparing the line and setting, the captain paced up and down the deck, berating the men. He was repeatedly explaining to us that Captain Timm was gone and that he was in charge. He spoke to us like we were little children who had tracked mud into the house. By the time the seat was ready, the captain had calmed noticeably, and it appeared his anger had abated. The lad was lashed to the seat, and the lines were made ready. At this point, we all, including Peter, believed this was just a simple lesson, and we assumed the boy would be quickly dunked once or twice as a reminder. As Peter was swung out over the water, he had a smile on his face.

"The captain gave the order to play out the line. The sailors did so slowly, so that young Peter was splashed by several waves before he settled in the water. Due to the movement of the ship through the water, Peter was sometimes under and sometimes half out of the water. It's often like this and is kind of a game, all in fun. Then the captain ordered him to be lowered to a full dunking.

Which the men did, and after no more than twenty seconds, the captain ordered them to haul in the line. I believe that would have been it except that as Peter broke the surface he was laughing and the men on deck were smiling and offering jibes at the young lad and one of the sailors, I don't know which, called out in a mirthful voice to the captain, 'If I call you Captain Timm can I go for a ride?' Instantly, everything changed. The captain visibly shook and screamed, 'Lower the line to a deep dunk!'.

"The men complied. The captain stepped to the rail and gazed out to sea, seeming to ignore everything. He left the boy down for a long time, too long, and we all knew it, but were afraid to act. All of us but your foolish friend. Derrick never said a word; he just went to the line and started to haul it in to raise the lad out of the water, hard work for one man alone, but I think he might have pulled Peter out in time if the captain hadn't grabbed a belaying pin and bashed him on the back of the head.

"The captain then returned to his station, looking off in the distance. By the time the captain gave the order for the men to haul in the line, we all knew it was too late. No sooner had the lad's body been removed from the seat than the captain ordered Derrick to be lashed to it. You know the rest."

Father Lull asked, "What happens now? Is Mary in any trouble? What are you going to do about the captain?"

Jacques said, "Mary has nothing to fear from me. I only wish I had acted as she and Derrick did. If I had, Peter might still be alive. If Raphael regains consciousness, we will hold a shipboard tribunal regarding his actions. I will preside over the trial as the new captain, and we will convict and sentence Raphael to a keelhauling or being tossed overboard with his hands and legs tied, or some other punishment which will undoubtedly result in his death. A fair exchange for young Peter. And I will take charge, and we will continue our voyage."

Father Lull asked, "And what is the destination of that voyage?"

Captain Jacques said, "That, I'm afraid, is the same destination that Captain Raphael had established. Although we were not fond of Raphael as our captain, his plan seemed like a good one to those of us who knew about it, and by now, I'm sure most of the crew know what was planned. If I choose to change the plan, I am certain I'd be ousted as captain. Besides, I also approved of the plan. You need to understand, we are not Templars, and although technically the Templars own this ship and we are just hired hands, once the ship is at sea, the captain controls the ship.

"Many on this crew have served for several years and sailed many long leagues under the Templar flag, and we have been paid fairly, but none of us grows rich, not even the captain. Captain Timm was very fond of the Templars and believed in their cause; he also greatly respected Admiral Gregory. The same can't be said for many of the crew. Some of the crew believe what is being said about the Templars, and others, like me, just don't know what to believe. None of us wants to be arrested and questioned by the Inquisition when we are only hired workmen. We look at what is in our hold and see a future that we could never attain by legal means. We envision a future where we no longer have to work until the day we die. A future with a wife and children and a home by the sea. As we see it, it's just not worth the risk to continue to sail for a group that seems to have somehow angered the King of France and the Holy Roman Church. We are not going to the meeting place; instead, we will head to Amsterdam, where we will pick up water, food, and other supplies, and then depart. I'll not tell you where unless you choose to come with us, and then only after we have sailed away from Amsterdam. I don't want any other ships trying to chase us down. I will tell you this about our destination: it is a wonderful place to start a new life. You are welcome to join us. We will share the wealth fairly with you, and you can live like princes for the rest of your days. If you choose not to join us, we will leave you in Amsterdam with enough coin to find passage aboard another ship. Just don't try to follow us. We view the treasure below as ours, and we will defend it."

Father Lull said, "The items below deck are not yours. If you steal the cargo that resides in the hold of the ship, this Templar ship, you will regret it for as long as you live, even if you live the life of a prince. No good will come of stealing what rightfully belongs to the Templars."

Mary had never seen the father so angry, even though he never raised his voice; he shook with rage. Mary, for one, could understand what the sailors intended; she didn't agree with them, but she could understand. She found it strange that she, who had been filled with anger when they had no idea where they were headed, seemed only slightly annoyed by this plan of the sailors. But now that they knew where the ship was heading, she felt better, while Father Lull was enraged.

They all seemed to forget about Derrick until he finally spoke. He tried to process his thoughts and determine what to say, but he had trouble finding the words. He seldom felt the need to speak. He believed that most of the time when people spoke, they were only speaking to hear themselves, and it served little purpose, but now he felt a wave of unaccustomed anger rise up in him, compelling him to say something. After some thought, he finally said in a low voice, "The Father is right. It is dishonorable to take what does not belong to you. A man can only truly enjoy that which he works and toils to attain."

Captain Jacques said, "I'm sorry you feel that way. Perhaps it would be best if you kept those opinions to yourself. We will be in Amsterdam the day after tomorrow if the wind holds. Once we arrive, I would ask that you remain below deck until we are ready to depart. At which time, I will have you taken ashore with enough money to continue to wherever you choose."

Chapter 40

It had been a couple of days since the fight with the other Scottish men loyal to Comyn.

After dinner, Louis wandered off by himself to walk along the river. He was a little confused by all the attention he had received since the battle. He couldn't recall doing anything particularly heroic or any great feat of arms, yet everyone treated him as if he were a famed warrior. He was also a little conflicted by his feelings after the battle. It had been bloody and chaotic, and his memories of it were confusing; a lot of what seemed to be becoming his memory of the conflict wasn't really what he could recall. A great deal of the gaps seemed to be getting filled in by what others told him happened or what "must have happened." And some of it he knew was just himself filling in the blanks to fit the story as it was presently being told. He wasn't trying to make things up; it just seemed his mind was doing it of its own accord, trying to make sense of all the senselessness.

He decided he had walked far enough and should get back. He turned around and walked most of the way back to the town when he saw a group of four or five figures coming toward him. It was just dark enough that he couldn't tell who they were, but since they approached from the direction of the town, he wasn't particularly concerned, but all the same, he wished he'd have taken a war-hammer with him on this walk. Just as he was thinking these thoughts, he began to hear the voices of those approaching. The voices were clearly female, and although he couldn't make out what they were saying, they seemed happy and excited.

He was glad it was a group of women and not just one. Since the fight, it seemed almost every eligible woman in the town wanted to spend time with him. This was a problem he never thought he'd face. He'd spent many hours in bars when he could sneak out of the commandery in Paris, trying to convince some barmaid or any unattached female he could find to go off to a nice pile of hay with him, but it never happened; they always had some excuse to put him off. Now he was the one coming up with excuses. He wasn't sure why he felt this way; the lasses were all pretty enough, well, most of them. For some reason, it felt wrong, not in a guilty religious way, but just not right. He supposed it had to do with the fact that they were trying to get him to pay attention to them because of the men he had killed, and he wasn't sure how he felt about that.

As the group of women drew closer, it became apparent that they had come to find him. He called out to them, "Young maidens, whatever are you doing out here alone? A beast or a man or a man-beast might come upon you. What would you do then?"

One of the women jeered back at him, "We Scottish women are not as dainty and defenseless as those French lasses you are used to. We can take care of ourselves." Louis recognized the voice as Isla. Of all the unattached young ladies in the village, it seemed she was the only one who hadn't approached him with offers to warm his bed. Truth be told, Louis was unsure how he would respond if she had made an offer. She was the only one he would like to spend some time with. Since their walk back from the hilltop with the sheep a week or so ago, he had attempted to find her and speak with her, but she was always busy.

Another of the group added with laughter in her voice, "I could take care of you, too, if you give me a chance."

The others all laughed at this until Isla said, "There will be no more of that talk. We were sent to carry out a duty, and that's what we will do." The laughter abruptly stopped.

As Louis met up with the group, the ladies all gathered around him, and Isla said, "We have been sent to fetch you back to the town and see that you take a proper bath. Others are preparing warm water as we stand here, so let's hurry so that their hard work does not go to waste."

Two of the young ladies took him by the arm and started leading him back to the town. Louis, letting himself be guided by the young ladies, said, "A bath? Why am I being taken back for a bath?"

Isla said, "I'm not sure of the customs where you come from, but here most people take a bath because their odor has grown unacceptable, and for the sake of the community, we try not to offend others with our smell."

Louis said, "I just took a bath in the river two days ago."

Isla said, "It is not for me to judge. Orders were given to prepare a bath and for us to fetch you, and that is what we are doing."

"Who gave those orders?" Louis became more confused by the moment. He was suddenly fearful that someone had decided he should be married, and this was in preparation for a forced wedding.

Isla replied, "These orders come from the King himself."

Now Louis was even more worried. He knew Robert the Bruce, King of Scotland, was in the town but hadn't even glimpsed Him. He had heard that King Robert was ill, and Louis assumed that this was the reason he had never seen him in the town.

Within a few minutes, they arrived at the town, and Louis was led by his female entourage to the church near the center of the village. There, just outside the church, were many people; to Louis, it looked like the whole town was present. A tent had been set up outside the church. Louis was directed inside, where he found William and Cinead. Cinead told Louis in a gruff voice, "Strip and get in the water, while it's still warm."

Louis looked at William and said, "Sir William, what in the world is going on? Did I do something wrong?"

William, looking somewhat angry, said, "You best do as you are told; otherwise, Cinead is likely to bring those young ladies back in here to strip and wash you."

Louis quickly disrobed and climbed into the tepid water. He had just settled into a seated position, his knees pulled up almost to his chest in the small make-shift tub, when Isla entered the tent. She looked at the three men in the tent as if challenging them to tell her to leave. None spoke. Isla tossed a brownish fist-sized object to Louis and said, "Use that to scrub yourself clean."

Louis looked at the object and asked, "What is it?"

Isla said, "It's goat fat and wood ash mixed with a little heather. It will help clean some of the grime off you." With that, Isla left.

Louis looked at the object for a moment, then shrugged and started to rub it on his arms. As he did this, he asked William, "Sir William, please, what is happening? This doesn't feel like I'm in trouble, but I do feel like you are setting me up for something."

William looked at Louis as if he felt sorry for him and said, "This is a matter of your own making. I can do nothing to rescue you from this fate. You need to find the courage and bear it yourself."

Louis stopped scrubbing and looked from William to Cinead, his eyes wide, "Sir William, Sir Cinead, what is going on? You're not marrying me off, are you? I believe I should…"

Cinead interrupted Louis in an explosion of voice, "WHAT ARE YOU SAYING? ARE OUR WOMEN NOT GOOD ENOUGH FOR YA?!"

Louis stammered out, "No, no. I'm not saying anything like that, the women here are great, their beautiful, and lively, and they speak their mind, I would be honored…"

Cinead interrupted again, "Good! Now that that is settled, finish your bath. After you are done washing, put on the robe laid out on the stool there. We will wait outside."

Before Louis could say anything more, Cinead and William left the tent. A moment later, Cinead stuck his head back in and said, "Stay away from my daughters, or I'll eat your gizzard for breakfast."

Louis hurriedly finished cleaning himself and put on the simple white robe Cinead had indicated. He stepped out of the tent into the now full darkness of the night. Many of the people of the town were still present, and there seemed to be a party atmosphere that abruptly faded away as he stepped out of the tent. William, Cinead, and the local Priest stood there waiting for him. William said, "Follow me."

The priest holding a candle led the way as William, then Louis, and Cinead trailed him quietly into the Church. It was very dark, the only illumination coming from the priest's lone candle. The Priest walked to the front of the Church and made the sign of the cross, and without turning to face Louis, he said, "Louis, please

171

kneel and examine your soul. We will leave you with God. I will return in one hour to hear your confession. Please be thorough." Then the priest placed the candle on the altar, and the three left the Church.

Louis was so overwhelmed by what was happening, he couldn't think straight for some time, so he repeated some prayers from memory. As the cadence and familiarity of the prayers continued, he began to sense the old feeling of calm and the presence of God as he knelt in the quiet, darkened Church.

Soon enough, the Priest returned and, after hearing the most honest confession Louis had ever given, the priest gave him a lengthy list of prayers of contrition, then he left. William and Cinead then reentered the church and knelt beside Louis. They spent the remainder of the night that way, kneeling, or sometimes lying flat on their faces, praying. Louis now knew what was happening and spent a good part of the night struggling with the commitment he knew he would be asked to make in the morning. It was not until just before sun-up that Louis resolved himself to the choice he would soon be forced to make.

As the sun rose, the three men stiffly got to their feet. Sir William turned to Louis and said, "Have you fully considered the commitment you are shortly going to be asked to make before God and man?"

Louis looked William full in the eyes and replied, "Yes, I have.'

William then asked more formally, "Louis de Champagne, is your answer resolutely on your heart, mind, and lips, and are you ready to make your answer known to both God and man?"

Louis replied, "Yes."

The three men left the Church, although William and Louis had to slow the pace for Cinead, who clearly had not spent that much time on his knees in a long time, if ever.

As they stepped out of the Church into the bright sunlight of early morning, the three men had to squint after being in the dark Church for so long. They made their way silently through the empty village to the main meeting hall. As they approached, Louis could see many people waiting outside. The villagers parted for the trio as they made their way to the door. Sir William opened the door and stood aside to allow Louis to enter first. The hall was filled with people. They stood on either side, leaving an aisle in the middle of the hall. At the far end of the hall, on a slightly raised platform, was a chair covered in furs, and seated on the chair was a man in his mid-thirties. Louis walked resolutely forward toward the man seated at the front with William and Cinead following. Louis walked with his eyes fixed on the man he knew must be Robert the Bruce, King of Scotland. The King's hair was darker than most Scots, his shoulders were very broad, and the man had a powerful build even while seated. His skin was slightly sallow, as though he had recently been ill, but his gaze was clear, intense, and penetrating.

When Louis reached the raised platform, he knelt before the King and bowed his head, exposing the back of his neck. King Robert then rose and stepped forward to the edge of the platform and said in a clear, loud voice, "Has this man been properly cleansed in body and spirit?"

The local priest who stood next to the chair the King had just vacated said, "He has, Your Majesty."

King Robert asked, "Who vouches for this man's honor and integrity?"

Sir William said, "I do, Your Majesty."

King Robert then asked, "Who vouches for this man's skill at arms?"

Sir Cinead said, "I do, Your Majesty."

King Robert asked, "Who vouches that this man has demonstrated understanding of heraldry, horsemanship, courtly etiquette, strategies in warfare, and all other aspects of a knight?"

Sir William said, "I do, Your Majesty."

King Robert then focused His attention on the kneeling Louis and asked, "Louis de Champagne, is your desire today to become a member of the chivalry?"

Louis raised his head so that he was looking up at King Robert the Bruce and said, "I do so desire, Your Majesty."

King Robert said to Louis, "As a knight, you will have a great deal of responsibility to God, the Church, your Lord, and to the people you are sworn to protect. You must always defend a lady, speak only the truth, and be devoted to the Church. You must be charitable and defend the poor and helpless. You must always be brave and be ready to lay down your life to protect others. When on a quest, you are never to remove your arms and armor except while sleeping. You can never avoid a dangerous path out of fear, and when you return to your Lord's court from an adventure, you must always tell of your escapades. If you are taken prisoner, you will surrender your horse and arms to your opponent and not fight the opponent again without his consent. Do you, Louis de Champagne, swear to uphold these ideals?"

Louis said, "I do, Your Majesty."

King Robert the Bruce then stepped down off the platform and stood directly in front of Louis and said, "Stand, Louis de Champagne."

Louis was confused. As he had witnessed knighting ceremonies many times, it was at this time that the Lord performing the rite would touch a sword to both shoulders of the man being knighted and then tell him to rise as a knight in the sight of God and man. He wondered briefly if something had happened, and he was not going to be knighted. Cinead then interrupted his thoughts by kicking him in the foot and said under his breath, "Get to your feet." Louis quickly stood.

King Robert then said, "Let this be the last blow you receive without responding." Before Louis could even think, King Robert struck Louis with a powerful open-handed blow on the left side of his face. Louis stumbled to the side and went down to one knee. He knelt there for a moment, trying to regain his senses.

King Robert then placed his left hand on Louis' shoulder and held out His right hand for Louis to take. Louis took the offered hand, and as King Robert the Bruce pulled Louis to his feet, he said, "Rise, Sir Louis de Champagne." Sir Louis would have been able to hear the people cheering better if it hadn't been for the ringing in his ears.

King Robert, still clasping Louis by the hand, waited for the crowd to quiet and said, "We will now hold a tournament of games in honor of this man becoming a member of the Chivalry, followed by a celebratory feast.

The Tournament was not like the ones Louis had attended in France, where only knights could participate. Here, anyone could join in, and some of the games involved teams where individuals seemed to change sides at will. What really surprised Louis, and all the other Templars, was that many of the women participated in some of the games.

One of the games was like a team version of Maglio. In Maglio, individuals competed by hitting a wooden ball with a wooden mallet through a high arch of iron, a long distance away, using the fewest strikes. In the Scottish version, there was a hole dug at each end of a field. The field was perhaps 500 feet long, and teams tried to knock the wooden ball with mallets, or just plain sticks, into the hole at one end or the other, depending on which team they were on. There was a great deal of tripping and full-body slams, with the team stealing the ball from the opposing team. This was one of the games that many of the women participated in.

At the feast, Louis asked Cinead about the blow Robert the Bruce had struck him. Cinead replied, "That's how we do it here. You took the blow well; there have been many times we had to wait a while for the freshly knighted individual to regain consciousness before the King could help him up, but the King has been sick lately; perhaps his strength has diminished a bit. Or maybe he was afraid to break your fragile French jaw."

Chapter 41

Henry sat in disbelief as Father Thomas told him all that had happened with Odo. When he finished, Henry said, "Your Eminence, this is why I can never trust Father Thomas. He must be lying about Odo. I have known Odo for several years, and he would not betray the Templar Order as Father Thomas would have us believe."

Cardinal Soprano said, "I believe you have witnessed, once strong men, knights in your Order, break under the pressure of torture or even just the threat of torture. I have read the accounts of what Odo had said before his death. Although I do not accept the truth of what Odo claimed to have witnessed and experienced, I believe he made the statements. We have collaborating accounts from sources outside of Brother Jaye's circle of influence. But as Father Thomas has indicated, your squire, Odo, may have become confused and not have been able to distinguish truth from fantasy because of physical or spiritual suffering."

Henry said, "I still don't believe it. Maybe he would have confessed to spitting on the cross or some other nonsense that the inquisition pressured him to admit, but the other lies of us worshiping demons or the filth about relations between brothers he would never have concocted. There is also no way I would believe that Odo would kill himself. Odo was one of the most devout Catholics I have known; it would never cross his mind to commit such a mortal sin."

Cardinal Soprano replied, "I cannot force you to believe what Father Thomas has said, but I challenge you to think it over. If you can read, and you wish to, I can have some of the documents brought to you to read for yourself. As for the poor boy killing himself, it is difficult to know what is in a man's heart, especially if he is troubled, as it appears Odo certainly was."

Cardinal Soprano then said, "Moving on to your other question, Sir Henry. We in the Cardinals' college have been working to determine the best way to deal with the Templars we have been able to collect here, and those that are in a couple of other locations under our protection. Let me assure you that the Holy Father does not believe the accusations against the Templars, but there is little He can do publicly without it harming the Seat of Saint Peter among the French people. The King of France has made everything very difficult, and although many of the other Monarchs do not agree with King Philip, they are not willing to stand against him in this matter.

"King Philip and his lapdog Guillaume de Nogaret have spread a very carefully constructed net, and any overt effort made by the Pope or any of the other Monarchs in Europe would likely cause a backlash by the common people, who seem to have embraced the idea of evil residing in the Templar Order."

Henry said, "So we are just to be abandoned because those in power are afraid to act?"

Cardinal Soprano replied, "You are not abandoned. That is why we brought you here. Most of the Monarchs are willing to do what they can, but they will need to hold trials in their own country to show the Templars are innocent of what King Philip is claiming. Denis I King of Portugal and His wife Queen Elizabeth of Aragon have allowed many of the Templars who have been able to escape settle there, and there is talk of re-establishing the Order in Portugal, perhaps under a different name."

Henry said, "And what is the Pope doing? He is supposed to be the only one we Templars answer to. Why has he not forced Philip to release the Templars he is holding prisoner? I think the Holy Father is overestimating the reaction of the people. If he had seen the response of the people of Paris when we confronted the King, He would see that the people are behind us."

Cardinal Soprano replied, "The common people are a finicky lot; they may support you one day, then call for your head the next. It all depends on who they heard most recently. We need to build a case at least as strong as King Philip's before we can risk speaking in favor of the Templars openly."

Henry asked, "What am I and my companions who came here supposed to do? Are we to work as kitchen help until you feel the case is strong enough?"

Cardinal Soprano said, "No, we have a plan in the works, and we are going to send you, your friends, and Father Thomas to the newly established Swiss Confederacy. As we can retrieve more of your brothers, we will send them your way."

"What and where is the Swiss Confederacy?" Henry asked.

Chapter 42

Captain Raphael recovered consciousness later the same day as the events that led to the death of young Peter. Mary, Derrick, and Father Lull remained below deck during the brief trial, which took place up on deck. They could hear voices raised in anger as things progressed. Then there were the sounds of a scuffle and more yelling mixed with quite a lot of laughing. Suddenly, there was a loud splash. A few minutes later, some of the men came below deck with the new Captain. Captain Jacques said, "It is finished. Captain Raphael has paid the price for killing young Peter and trying to kill Derrick. I am in command of this vessel. I wanted to ask you three one last time, do you still intend on getting off in Amsterdam, or would you like to join us?"

Father Lull instantly replied, "No. We have no desire to join with individuals who would steal just because they see an opportunity."

Captain Jacques said, "I am sorry you feel that way, Father. We do not see it as stealing. When we arrive in Amsterdam, we will take on supplies, and you three will remain below deck. Once we are ready to depart, I will have a couple of men row you three ashore."

Captain Jacques thought one of the three would make some reply, but he received only an awkward silence, so he finally said, "If you need anything, send one of the men to find me." Then he left.

Mary said to Father Lull, "Father, I realize it's wrong for them to take what belongs to the Templars, but I don't think it helps to be so harsh. These men are simply taking the opportunity to better their lot in life. I don't agree with their decision, but I understand it."

Father Lull said, "I do not. The wealth in this ship represents far more lives than these few sailors. I don't guess there is anything we can do about it. The three of us won't be able to overpower them, and they won't let us alert the authorities in Amsterdam to stop them. It is just so frustrating that all this wealth, which was gained by great effort and loss of life, is simply going to sail away with men who have no idea of its true value."

The ship arrived in Amsterdam early in the morning, a couple of days after Captain Jacques took over. There was a lot of action on board as small boats rowed back and forth, bringing supplies to the ship. Mary, Derrick, and Father Lull saw none of this, but they heard it and witnessed the men bringing casks, crates, and other items below deck to be stowed away.

It was late afternoon when Captain Jacques appeared below deck and said, "It's time to take you ashore."

He led them up on deck and handed Mary a small pouch of money, saying, "Don't worry, none of this money is from the hold, so you can spend it with a clear conscience. I assume there's no reason to ask if you've changed your mind and wish to join us, so I will just say good-bye."

Father Lull and Derrick said nothing, but Mary said, "Thank you for the money." She wanted to wish them good luck but felt Derrick and Father Lull would be irritated if she offered anything that could be seen as encouragement. Father Lull, who had always been so friendly and always laughing and talking, had been very subdued and on edge since they had learned about the plans of the sailors to take the ship and the treasure in its hold.

The rowboat deposited them as the sun was nearing the horizon. The three stood on the small dock watching the rowboat head back to the ship, where it was hoisted on deck. The ship raised sail and departed into the setting sun. The only sound was the water slapping against the dock and seagulls circling overhead.

As the ship receded into the distance, Father Lull suddenly said in his old upbeat voice, "Oh well. Let us see if we can't find ourselves a decent meal and a place to sleep for the night. In the morning, we will need to start looking for passage on a ship."

Mary asked, "How difficult will it be for us to find a ship to Germany?"

Father Lull replied, "Oh, we're not going to look for a ship to Germany. Lehe, Germany, was just supposed to be a stopover for us to resupply and carry out any maintenance on the ships if need be.

We are looking for a ship to Bergen, Norway. I assume we should be able to find a berth on a trader easily. I pray the other two ships arrive in Bergen safely. That's in God's hands now as far as my involvement is concerned anyway."

Chapter 43

Sir Henry de Créon and Sir Garrard de La Longuedoc rode at the front of a line of about a hundred men; about half of the group were Templars like themselves, although none wore any device to indicate that they were anything other than swordsmen or knights acting as guards to the rest of the group. The rest of the company was made up of priests, servants, tradesmen, and one cardinal. Directly behind Sir Henry and Sir Garrard rode Thomas the Priest and Cardinal Soprano, the two talking quietly while seated on horseback. The Cardinal refused to ride in a wagon, stating that he had spent many hours on horseback. Although Sir Henry was certain that it had been many years since the Cardinal had been in the saddle, after a few hours, it was clear his legs and backside were sore.

Sir Henry looked over his shoulder and then returned his gaze forward as he said to Sir Garrard, "I do not trust that Priest. I think he has fooled Cardinal Soprano. This mission that the Holy Father has asked us to undertake is risky enough without including a snake like Father Thomas."

Sir Garrard replied, "I understand your reluctance in trusting that Father Thomas has indeed changed. And I agree we should keep an eye on him. Yet I find it hard to believe that Cardinal Soprano would be taken in if the priest were false. I have heard some things about the Cardinal, and he is not your typical prince of the Catholic Church."

Henry was just about to ask what Sir Garrard had heard when Cardinal Soprano asked the two knights, "Do you suppose we could stop for a bit and stretch our legs? I have not ridden a horse for so long in many years, and I believe I have lost feeling in my lower half."

Sir Garrard halted his horse, turned around in his saddle, and said, "By all means. We can water the horses and get a bite to eat ourselves."

They halted the caravan of horses, donkeys, and the few wagons in a clearing that was edged by woods. The cardinal eased himself slowly out of the saddle and took several steps, slightly hunched over, before he could stand fully erect. The Cardinal said to no one in particular, "Nope, I haven't lost feeling in my legs; my inner thighs feel like they are on fire. I need to walk." The Cardinal then drew a six-foot-long walking stick from his gear, and he and Father Thomas walked off toward the tree line. The rest of the men busied themselves with watering the horses and eating some bread they had prepared for the trip.

As they strolled slowly and stiffly, away from the others, Cardinal Soprano stretched his back and used the walking stick to lean on. He said to Thomas, "My ass is completely numb, and yet I have stabs of pain up the back of my legs to my lower back. You may find it hard to believe, but years ago, I nearly lived in the saddle. I suppose I'll get used to it before we reach our destination." After a brief pause, where the Cardinal bent forward and touched the ground with his fingertips, he added, "I don't believe Sir Garrard trusts you yet."

Thomas said, "I wouldn't trust me either. Honestly, I'm not sure I trust myself. There were times in my past where I wanted to be the man you seem to think I can become, but experience tells me I will fail."

Cardinal Soprano said, "All have sinned and fallen short of the Glory of God. Neither God nor I expects you to be perfect. You will stumble, but if you keep God before you, if you commit your life to glorify God, you will make the right choices… mostly."

"I have spent most of my life looking out for myself. Sir Henry was not far off when he said I would do whatever it takes to survive. The only good things I have done have been performed either because I was told by my superiors or because I thought I would benefit from it." Thomas said.

The two men had about reached the trees, and Cardinal Soprano stopped and placed a hand on Thomas' shoulder and said, "Father Thomas, I know you can change. You may suppose you are exceedingly evil and cannot be redeemed, but I know from personal experience that you are wrong on both counts. Additionally, if you suppose any of us does good deeds for purely selfless reasons, you are foolish. I do good because it makes me feel closer to God, and that makes the act somewhat selfish, but that is a longer and deeper discussion we will have to save for later. Now we should return to the others."

As the two men turned their backs to the woods and started to walk back, Cardinal Soprano said in a low voice, "Don't look back or change your pace, but there are men in the woods. I saw at least ten, and they are armed."

Father Thomas replied, his eyes a little wide in fear, "Surely they won't attack us with all these armed men in our company?"

Just then, several men stepped out of the tree line. One of the men called in a loud voice, "Your Eminence, if you would kindly halt. I mean none of you any harm, but I am honor-bound to tell you I have a company of archers in the woods on both sides of the road and about fifty knights and sergeants with their complement of squires. You all appear to be well-equipped to handle yourself, but I believe we would win if you chose to fight. Again, let me emphasize we mean your company no harm. We just need information and a hostage to guarantee we get the truth."

The man then waved two of his men forward and continued, "Your Eminence, these two young men are my personal squires; they mean you no harm, but if you and the good Father would kindly accompany them back here to the woods until our negotiations are over…"

At that moment, the two squires got within about three feet of the Cardinal, who suddenly spun his walking stick in his right hand and then up over his head with both hands. Then before either squire could raise their swords, which they had kept pointed at the ground, the Cardinal struck one of them a crushing blow on top of the head. The Cardinal then took a step to the side and reversed the angle of the walking stick in a sideways strike that caught the other squire on the side of the head. Both squires were dropped to the ground unconscious before anyone could react or say a word. The Cardinal then planted his walking stick back on the ground and said, "I think I will remain here."

Sir Henry announced loudly, "Sir, I don't know who you think you are…" but before he could continue, he was cut off by someone clapping his hands together loudly. He looked to his side to see Sir Garrard clapping with a wide smile across his face.

Sir Garrard looked directly at the man who had sent his squires to retrieve the two holy men, and said, "It appears your squires need further training Sir Gilbert de Lyon."

The other man gawked for a moment as if his brain was trying to wake up from a dream, then he said, "Sir Garrard? Is that you?"

Sir Gilbert soon had his men out of the woods, and both groups came together as long-lost family members. Food was retrieved from the wagons of Sir Henry's group and greedily consumed by Sir Gilbert's men.

Sir Gilbert, Sir Henry, Sir Garrard, Cardinal Soprano, and Father Thomas met a little apart from the others. Sir Gilbert appeared nearly overwhelmed with joy at having met fellow Templars. He said to them, "So, it has all been false? Haven't all the Templars been arrested? We thought we were the only ones left and have been trying to return to France for months."

Cardinal Soprano said, "It is not all false, most of the Templars in France and some beyond have been arrested. These people here in this group had all previously been arrested by King Philip and are now escaping. You should join our band."

Sir Garrard said, "Sir Gilbert, where have you been? What are you doing here?"

Sir Gilbert said, "It is a long story. I was sent in command of these men to retrieve some Templar property on an island near Ethiopia. We were sailing aboard five ships hired by the Grand Master, and we put in at Naples to resupply and refit. It was there that we started hearing rumors of the arrest and imprisonment of Templars. We left Naples, and most of us considered it just a rumor and exaggeration. At worst, a misunderstanding that would soon be sorted out. Our hired ship master felt otherwise. A couple of days out of Naples, he came to me and said the drinking water and much of the food had gone bad, and said we would need to put into port on the island of Crete. He assured me the Venetians, who control the island, would see us properly fitted out in no time. Upon our flotilla's arrival in Crete, they had all of us rowed ashore while the Ship sat at anchor. No sooner than the last of us were ashore, the ships raised sail, weighed anchors, and left us ashore, taking all our supplies and the few horses we had brought.

"We spent several months trying to convince the Venetians to help us, but to no avail. Eventually, we convinced some local Cretan fisherman to ferry us across to a deserted spot on the toe of Italy. From there, we walked, avoiding major cities and trying to keep to ourselves.

"There really is little of interest left to the story until we stumbled upon you. And we would have stayed hidden in the woods until you passed except that when I saw you, you were traveling with a Cardinal. I couldn't pass up the opportunity to get some answers from someone high up in the Church. By the way, are you a real Cardinal? No offense, Your Eminence, but I've never seen a member of the clergy wheel a staff the way you did."

Cardinal Soprano replied, "Yes, my son. I am a real Cardinal. My ability with weapons is due to a misspent youth. Now, if you gentlemen will excuse me, I believe I will go check on your squires. I will let Sir Garrard and Sir Henry fill you in on what has transpired in France and what our current mission is. Before I go, Sir Gilbert, I only count about forty-five men total and don't see any archers. Where are the rest of your men?"

Sir Gilbert said, "Well, I may have exaggerated a bit. I have eleven knights and seven sergeants-at-arms; the rest are all squires. No archers, I'm afraid. I thought the threat of arrows raining down might give me enough time to talk with you and find out what is happening."

Chapter 44

The day following the knighting of Louis, Sir William was in a tent with Admiral Gregory, making final plans as the Templar fleet was about to depart. The ships were all loaded with supplies, and the men were making ready to embark. Louis arrived with Cinead at the tent, and they both entered. William and Gregory both stopped their conversation and looked at them. Admiral Gregory stepped to Louis and reached out to grip his forearm, saying, "Sir Louis, congratulations on your knighting. I rather enjoy the method the Scotts use to complete the ritual, although, for a moment, I was confused. I'm just glad it was barehanded. If the King had been wearing a gauntlet when he struck you, I'm afraid you wouldn't have recovered so quickly."

Louis responded, "Thank you, Admiral. I also was confused, although some of my confusion was because the Kings' blow had momentarily scrambled my brains."

Sir William said, "I guess I need to select another squire now. And come to speak of it, so do you. It may need to wait until we reach our next destination, as we hope to set sail in two days."

Louis looked at William and said, "That is partly what I came here to speak to you both about. I'm not going to continue with the fleet."

William looked quickly at Cinead, who raised a hand palm out, "This had nothing to do with me. I was sent here as the King's representative. Hear the lad out...sorry, hear the man out."

William then said to Henry, "I don't understand. As a Templar, there are not a lot of other choices that make sense. It would be foolish to return to France; I suppose you could stay here, but to what end?"

Louis said, "I agree if I had previously taken the vows of a Templar; it only makes sense that I would continue with you, but I am not a Templar."

William said, "That is easily resolved. Now that you are a knight, you just need to take the vows of our Order and become a warrior-monk of the Knights of the Temple."

Louis, in a slightly quieter voice, said, "I'm not sure of the truth of that. You are Templars because you have taken vows and made commitments to God, the Pope, and the Holy Church. Vows you cannot lay aside without leave from the Grand Master or by your death. Now things are different. Can I make a vow to a Pope who has all but abandoned the Order, or to a Church that seems to believe we are evil? Additionally, the entire purpose of the Order is changed. I was ready to sacrifice my life to protect pilgrims and fight the infidel for the Holy Lands, but now the fight is merely for survival in our homelands.

"Do you know why I so willingly chose to become a squire to the Templar Order? I had no desire to own land in Outremer. I was not simply sent to the Templars to learn the martial skills that only the Templars could offer to teach me. I have wanted to be a Knight Templar since I was six, when I heard a priest speak about the need for men to reclaim the lands of our Lord Jesus from the heathens. He told of the bravery of the Templars who count their life as lost and fight only to aid the poor pilgrims who cannot protect themselves. It was the first time I felt a calling to be more than just myself, which does not seem to be the goals of our Order any longer. Now the goal seems to be that of self-preservation; perhaps that will change in the future, but I don't think it will be anytime soon."

William said with a little anger in his voice, "This present situation is not permanent. Soon the Pope will prevail over King Philip, and we will return to our previous station and…"

Admiral Gregory interrupted, "Sir William, you need to listen to what this young Knight is telling you. He is speaking truths that most members of our Order are afraid to voice. Perhaps we have given too much and sacrificed too long to be able to face these facts, but for all our sake, we need to listen."

Louis continued calmly, "I have thought about it for a long time now, and these are the conclusions I've come to. I am uncertain there is an Order to make a commitment to. Even if the arrests had not taken place, I am uncertain I would still desire to become a Templar or any of the other warrior orders, since it appears unlikely any will return to the Holy Lands during my lifetime. I considered joining a purely ecclesiastical Order, but I don't see myself as a good priest or humble monk. I still feel a strong urge to go to the Holy Lands and free the homeland of Our Christ so that any Christian can safely walk the paths our Lord trod while on this Earth. During the feast last night, King Robert asked me about my plans, and I poured my heart out to Him as I am to you now."

William, still with an angry tone in his voice, said, "I assume He offered you a place among his knights fighting for Scotland."

Cinead, a glint of anger in his eyes, said, "I have not known you long, Sir William, but I consider you a friend, and I know this is hard for you, but do not insinuate any dishonor on my King."

William looked hard at Cinead, and then his glare softened, "I apologize. As you said, this is hard on me. I have grown to trust and respect Louis and have assumed he would be at my side during this difficult path I am forced to follow."

Cinead said, also in a calmer voice, "Show him that respect he earned and hear his words. He is wiser than he lets on. Clearly wiser than you or I, and perhaps more committed to his beliefs than most holy men I have known."

After a brief pause, William said, "Please continue, Louis."

Louis continued, "As I spoke with King Robert, I discovered, to my surprise, He also has a great desire to free the Holy Lands, as great a desire as I feel. He said that if it were not for the troubles here in Scotland, he would have chosen to go crusading if there was a crusade to join. He also stated that he would do everything in His power to raise a new crusade once he was firmly established and recognized by the other monarchs as the rightful King of Scotland.

"I told King Robert that I have heard about a Prester John in the Far East who has an army and fights for God, and my desire to seek him out. King Robert said he had heard the stories also and that many had sought him out, but nothing had ever come of it. I told the King that maybe I could succeed where others failed. He did offer to make me one of His knights, but not to fight for Scotland; rather, He wants me to lay the groundwork for a new crusade to retake the Holy Lands. He offered to pay for my voyage to the Holy Lands and beyond to seek the truth about Prester John. He said that I should come to you and ask your blessing to join His service. He also said to tell you and Admiral Gregory that, in exchange for my service, he would allow one of his knights to accompany you in my place for at least one year or until you grew tired of his service to you."

William was silent for a moment, then he said, "I would like to argue with you to change your mind, but I can see your mind is made up, and I don't know what I could say anyway. I will truly miss you, Sir Louis, even your persistent prattling on."

Gregory added, "Young knight, I believe you are making the right choice, but I would ask that you don't share your decision with the other Templars. We are facing difficult times ahead, and I would prefer that others do not question their vows any more than they already do. Now, what knight is the good King of Scotland blessing us with?"

Cinead replied, "An old warhorse, he said, was of no use to him anymore. They almost came to blows over it, but He is the King, and His will prevails."

Admiral Gregory grinned and said as he clapped Cinead on the shoulders, "I know this is not what you wanted, but I'm glad to have you along for as long as Robert can spare you. I'm sure with you, things will be more… colorful. I am sorry we are taking you from your family. Who will protect your daughter's virtue while you're gone?"

Sir Cinead said, "Have you seen my daughters? They look like something the cat dragged in after mauling it half to death. I need to find myself a rich blind man to take one of them off my hands. I kept trying to get young Sir Louis here to take an interest in one, but he wouldn't do it. He acted as if he were afraid of something."

Epilogue

As the ships set sail and began the voyage to Norway, Sir Louis was in his tent preparing his gear for his own far longer trip. He neatly laid out all the items that Robert, King of Scotland, had given to him after Louis swore fealty to Him. The items included: a new sword, a war-hammer, armor, spurs, a belt, a shield, and a surcoat with the King's lion rampant in red emblazoned on it. Before he placed any of these new and expensive items in the trunk, he carefully handled an old surcoat. This surcoat was frayed and had rust and bloodstains on it that Louis could not remove without destroying the well-worn cloth any further than it already was. The surcoat was emblazoned with a black Templar cross of a sergeant-at-arms. He placed it in a small wooden box he had made for this purpose. He then placed the box in the trunk and said to the box, "I'm sorry for how we left you, Sergeant Bertrand, but I promise I will lay your surcoat to rest in Jerusalem or die trying."

www.ingramcontent.com/pod-product-compliance
Lightning Source LLC
Chambersburg PA
CBHW072353190626
46811CB00019B/773